"Centers on the difficulties of living with family—immediate and extended, those related by marriage and by blood—and all the tricky, prone-to-misunderstanding nuances such relations entail."
—*Los Angeles Times*

"An earnest debut . . . a quietly competent collection."
—*Kirkus Reviews*

"Joann Kobin's stories do two things wonderfully: They create small, densely packed worlds, suffused with felt life and the sorts of insights you can't wait to jot down, and they also create leakages, channels running from one story to the next. I wanted to keep following Harriet: into the strains of advanced motherhood, into love, into sex, into food and longing and all the rich parts of her life. She's what a great fictional character should be: a little smarter than the rest of us, guiding us on a tour through the city of adult life." —Anthony Giardina, author of *Recent History*

"Worth reading, particularly for the opening story, 'Rain,' and the closing one, 'Discipline and Will,' both of which are masterfully written. It shows the cracks and pain beneath the surface of even the most normal-looking family, and how the emotional wounds from divorce can remain unhealed for years."
—*Austin American-Statesman*

"Joann Kobin's stories are unfailingly deft and observant, and the subtitle of the book they've been gathered into delivers on its promise. This really is 'a novel in stories,' a book with the momentum and expansiveness that few others in this tricky combination-genre can honestly claim." —Thomas Mallon

Woman Made of Sand

A NOVEL IN STORIES

Joann Kobin

BERKLEY BOOKS, NEW YORK

$\mathcal{B}$

A Berkley Book
Published by The Berkley Publishing Group
A division of Penguin Group (USA) Inc.
375 Hudson Street
New York, New York 10014

PRINTING HISTORY
Previously published by Delphinium Books in 2002
Berkley trade paperback edition / November 2003

Library of Congress Cataloging-in-Publication Data

Kobin, Joann.
Woman made of sand : a novel in stories / Joann Kobin.
p. cm.
Contents: Rain—Charity work—Dancing with time—What I learned from Clara—His mother, his daughter—Woman made of sand—Madonna at Monterchi—At the "Changing Careers" Conference—The provider—Chicken livers—Discipline and will.
ISBN 0-425-19182-6 (pbk.)
1. United States—Social life and customs—Fiction.
2. Domestic fiction, American. I. Title.

PS3611.O33 W66 2003
813'.6—dc21
2003044441

To my family, with love and appreciation

Contents

Woman Made of Sand

Joann Kobin

Rain

It never entered my mind that anyone in my husband's family would die. Certainly not my father-in-law. The Stedmans were healthy and fiscally responsible people with property and a business passed on from father to son. I thought they'd go on forever. There was a cushion of money. Not endless amounts, but a cushion. They seemed indestructible. Not like my family, which unraveled and foundered, produced only one child, mixed religions and uncertain genes, and then proceeded to die off rapidly. In the past ten years Roger hadn't grown old, he'd just grown leathery.

Friends and family gathered from all over for the funeral. Well-dressed people, but not flamboyant. People with good taste and expensive shoes. Women with real gold jewelry and name-brand leather handbags. Business associates and former secretaries. Friends from the condo. Funeral arrangements evolved thanks to some invisible committee of close relatives. No one person made any decisions. I know that Phillip, my husband, didn't. His mother didn't. His sister, Enid, didn't because she was en route from Seattle. I certainly didn't. But the casket was purchased and the funeral was arranged, as though there were an invisible impresario.

The memorial service in the funeral home's chapel struck me as false. I didn't like feeling that. I'm interested in the art of biography, and in a certain way eulogies fall into that category: how lives are explained, how they're gathered up and given shape; but some truthfulness is essential.

The minister was going on about Roger and his life, even though he'd met him only twice, and briefly at that. "A generous man," he proclaimed, and when he finished I watched Belle, Phillip's mother, accept friends' and relatives' overblown tributes, each a rose for a phony bouquet. *No*, I wanted to say, *he wasn't everybody's friend; no, he wouldn't give you the shirt off his back—or at least not without a price; no, he didn't always have a kind word for everybody; no, he didn't love life.* I remembered how quickly his joviality dissolved when no one was around to see it, how he sat holding a glass of Scotch and melted ice cubes and stared at us— the children and me, his son, too, sometimes his own wife, as though we were raggle-taggle relatives from some impoverished third-world country, waiting for a handout. In those deflated little moments I thought he disliked us. Bits of rage were exploding inside of me as if I had swallowed a time-release poison capsule.

I remembered a time some years ago when we went out to Huntstown to visit Roger and Belle in their new condo. All of us missed their old big white-frame house—with a fireplace, a screened-in porch, a barbecue grill in the backyard. I was wearing a silky white-and-red print jumpsuit on that summer afternoon, clingy and moderately low cut. Roger said, "Honey, that outfit looks terrific on you." He was checking me out from head to toe. The practiced way he did it made me realize he had an eye for the ladies and had probably acted on it plenty of times. But I was in the mood to appreciate what I believed was his lust, or his flirtatiousness, whatever. I was something of a flirt myself; besides, I was flattered. Phillip was working too hard to notice how I looked and he was mad at me because I wanted him to stand up to his father. I wanted him to work normal working hours; I wanted him to spend more time at home. Ever since we'd moved back from Richmond, Roger had a way of making Phillip feel he wasn't doing enough for the business, that Phillip wasn't loyal or committed enough, that profits were never good enough — although the business, a successful wallpaper company, was expanding with new offices in Dallas and San Francisco and an enormous sleek showroom planned for Chicago. They were making tons of money on durable, washable wallcoverings for hospitals and institutions.

Okay, so Roger thought I was a sexy dish that summer afternoon in Huntstown. I didn't mind and Phillip didn't seem to mind that his father was flirting with me. I hadn't had a father since I was eight and being paid attention to felt fine with me. Besides, there were times when I liked Roger's bluster: it felt like love to me, and maybe it was. However, a little while later when Roger and I found ourselves alone on the balcony, he stared off into the distance, his hooded eyes unseeing, indifferent. He was absolutely still. The sun was shining on him; he was as dry and scaly and silent as an iguana. I tried to find something to say, some statement or question, but I couldn't think of anything. Weather, baseball, news, local gossip. "How's Aunt Violet doing?" I finally asked. "Scraping along," he replied, and suddenly he jerked to life and reached around to his back pocket — oh, familiar motion — and lifted out his wallet. He stared at the happy thick wad and fished out five twenty-dollar bills and handed them to me. "Get yourself another outfit like the one you have on," he told me, then winked. Twice I refused the money, but he stood up and folded the bills and moved toward me and I thought he was going to slip the money down the front of my neckline but he stopped short of that. He pressed the bills into my hand. "Don't be foolish, Harriet. Never turn down good hard cash. Didn't anyone ever teach you that? Take it, say *thank you*, and then do whatever you want with it." He left the balcony and went inside.

I followed. "Look," I said, holding out the folded bills, "I can afford to buy my own clothes. . . ." As soon as those words were out of my mouth, I knew they were too cold, somehow irrelevant.

"Don't be childish," he said. "I know you can buy whatever you want, but I like how you look in that little suit, so get yourself another — on me — or a nightgown or something," and he wouldn't take back the money. I fumed, my face warming with anger, but I couldn't think of what to say. I wanted to be adorable *and* strong. I didn't want to have to choose one or the other. I shook my head and tried to slip the bills into Roger's shirt pocket, but he stepped out of my reach and laughed at me. Finally I put the money on one of Belle's mahogany end tables, and it sat there all afternoon at the base of a porcelain mermaid. Later, before we all went out to Roger's club for dinner, the money was still there, and Eric, our eleven-year-old son, wanted to know how come all that money was just lying there next to the mermaid. No one said anything. All I could think of was, *Where the hell is Phillip?*

I sat in the chapel between Eric and Phillip, who had drunk a few shots of his father's Chivas Regal before we left his parents' apartment, while Reverend Jarvis read a psalm, and suddenly excitement tremored up my spine. I wanted to get up and move. I wanted to march for miles behind a horse-drawn cart to the burial grounds. I couldn't wait to see that deep rectangular cut in the ground, that dark slot waiting patiently as a lover in bed, for the beloved. And it wasn't because I was happy that Roger was dead—but because of the fact that he *was*, and all the words spoken in this chapel were just words: they were beside the point. We needed the shovel, the earth, salty tears, a song.

We were in a long, black limousine that followed the hearse on and off Long Island's expressways and the main streets of its towns, a mazelike route to Evergreen Cemetery. Belle, Eric, and Matina, my sixteen-year-old daughter, and Phillip and myself, and Phillip's sister, who had flown in alone from Seattle. The force that had always held us together was Roger, and he wasn't there. For the first time since I'd heard the news of his death I truly missed him. He made me feel safe, don't ask me why, I don't know why. I said, "Dad should be sitting here with us." No one agreed or disagreed. Phillip was mute. We were borne along now by the hired officials of funeral land.

I gazed out the window. Clouds that had been fluffy and white darkened and multiplied, but perhaps I was simply viewing the sky through the smoky tinted glass of the Cadillac's windows. Out of respect for the dead we moved more slowly than the rest of traffic, although the hearse had long since disappeared. None of the cars in the cortege was in view. We were heading to a part of Long Island that I didn't know. The driver sneaked a look at a map that he had unfolded on the seat next to him.

Phillip said, "I hope Reverend Jarvis finds his way to the cemetery."

"Of course he will," Enid reassured. "He must go there often enough." She spoke keeping her wonderful green eyes closed. Actually her eyes had been closed since she'd gotten into the limo. She opened them only to light her cigarettes. Smoke filled the car. Matina, who at sixteen can be bossy, told her aunt that she shouldn't be smoking in such a small enclosed space. I heard Enid mutter under her breath, "Oh shut up, Matina." The driver took the next exit off the expressway only to make his way back on, heading in the opposite direction.

Eric twisted around and touched his grandmother's hand. At eleven he was still incredibly sweet. I saw that he wanted to take her hand and hold it and offer her comfort. Belle hadn't noticed the children's solicitude to her from early morning on, and now said—to no one in particular—"I've lost my best friend." That unruly voice inside of me murmured, *your only friend.*

"Grandpa always had beautiful ties," Matina reminisced.

"He liked silk ties," Belle said. "He liked nice things—but he wasn't a dandy-type. He was a man you could lean on." *You sure leaned,* I wanted to say. And I wanted to say more. I wanted to say, *Belle, now would be the perfect moment to tell Matina that she could have one or two of her grandfather's beautiful ties.* Matina, on occasion, liked wearing men's ties and shirts. But, of course, Belle wasn't thinking about Matina or Eric, for that matter, or anybody except herself. I was dissatisfied with what everyone said and did. I was impatient, angry, bossy—in my head, at least.

"Anyone for a spearmint leaf?" I asked. I had found a small cellophane bag of the green candies in my pocketbook. Eric was the only one who nodded. Belle said, "No thank you." Her voice was crisp.

Phillip didn't want a spearmint leaf either. He glanced at me accusingly. "You know," he said in a hushed whisper, "I've been thinking back on the past years and trying to figure out why we ever moved away from Huntstown. What made us trot off to Virginia? And why didn't we move back to Huntstown instead of to Manhattan?" His voice was thankfully low.

I was caught off guard by his questions. "We wanted to try a different kind of life," I whispered, leaning toward him, hoping to feel the warm heft of his body but instead feeling only layers of clothing. "We wanted some adventure." He didn't respond and as usual I continued, even though I knew I shouldn't: I was trying to learn not to fill silences, but to bear them. I was trying to learn that there wasn't an answer for every question or a reason for every decision. I wanted to believe that he understood our life in the same ways I did. But I couldn't stop myself from reminding him that he was the one who wanted to try working for someone besides his father. "That's what *you* wanted," he murmured. "I was happy with the way things were. I liked living close to my folks." Matina settled her eyes on us, but Phil didn't notice. I straightened, stung by his words.

Because I knew at some level that what he said was true. I believed so much in *becoming*, in possibility, that I looked at others with a critical eye, waiting impatiently for them to become who I thought they should become. And Phillip had gone along with me. Or did I drag him along, pull him like a heavy stone? Or was I always pushing him, pushing him to places he didn't want to go? I was never sure what he wanted. Where did he *want* to go?

In a few moments Phillip forgot about me. "My father never had an unkind word to say about anybody," he said aloud, and I thought, *But he never had a kind word to say about anyone.* "I should have insisted that he work only one or two days a week,"

Phillip confessed seconds later to his sister. "He was a man in his seventies and he was working too hard—and he was overeating."

"It's not your fault that Dad died, Phil," Enid said crossly. "Don't be so vainglorious." I thought, *Hooray!*

"I've lost my best friend," Belle murmured again.

Enid said, "Ma, don't worry, you have us." *Yeah*, I thought, *you'll be a big help from Seattle.*

I was rewriting the script, a mean-spirited one.

Then Belle wrote her own line: "I don't need anyone to help me. I'll be okay." Again her tone was crisp. That was the source of her pride: not needing anything.

The limo was traveling faster now, speeding past other cars, moving into a less populous area of Long Island. I rolled down my window a couple of inches. The sky had turned into an ocean, the earth had flipped over. Rough gray clouds filled the sky; they seemed to be getting lower and lower, as though soon they'd press down on top of the limo and flatten us.

"Harriet, what kind of platters did you order?" Enid asked, opening her eyes. I was grateful to hear my name. "Turkey and ham, tuna salad, cut-up vegetables." She closed her eyes and murmured, "Good."

"Are there any paper plates and cups in the house?" I asked Enid, but before she could answer, Belle said, "I can't deal with a crowd."

"Don't you want the family to come back with us, Mom?"

"I don't care."

"When are we going to get to the cemetery?" Eric asked.

"We're lost," Belle said matter-of-factly.

Then I realized that Belle was, of course, right. The driver was going around in circles. We'd passed the same run-down shopping center three times. Finally he pulled into a gas station and asked for directions. While he was talking to the attendant, it began to rain.

Enid stared at her mother. "What do you mean 'you don't care,' Mom?"

"Exactly what I said: I don't care. Invite anyone or no one. I don't care."

There was a long line of cars waiting for us when we arrived at the cemetery; the hearse, at the head of the line. We moved to the head of the line, right behind the hearse. A man with an umbrella tapped on Belle's window. It was Reverend Jarvis. A breath of fresh air blew in when Belle lowered her window, a sweet mixture of earth and rain, more like early spring than fall. The minister said, "Belle, we were getting worried about you. Are you all right?" He smiled at her and glanced at the rest of us, the smile fading as he shifted his umbrella and looked up at the sky. "There's going to be a downpour. Just a minute, I'll be back." He went off to confer with two men in dark overcoats.

"Where's Grandpa?" Eric asked. No one answered—I think because no one in the car was sure whether the casket was still in the hearse or whether it had been moved to the grave.

The driver got out of the limo. Belle's elderly brother, Uncle Gordon, handsome old walrus, appeared and tapped on her window. "Let's try to do the service before the storm," he told his sister. "What took you so long?"

"Uncle Gordie is right," I said. "We better have the burial before it comes down even harder."

"Mom doesn't have a raincoat," Phillip said.

Enid lit a cigarette and closed her eyes. "Please, Enid," I said, "could you not smoke in here now?" She took a deep drag and without looking at me tapped the cigarette out in the ashtray in front of Eric, who was looking through a pack of baseball cards.

Reverend Jarvis returned and beckoned Phillip. With some reluctance Phillip stepped out of the limo. They stood talking a couple of yards away, their heads pivoting—from the direction of the grave site back to us. I got out of the car and joined them. Reverend Jarvis ordered me back to the limo. "It's raining, Audrey." "I'm Harriet," I told him, but he seemed too rattled to care. I asked Phil what was going on. "The rain," Phillip explained, "Reverend Jarvis thinks Mom may get too upset when she sees the casket lowered into the grave." "But now is the time to get upset," I said. "There are times to get upset, and this is one of them. Her husband of almost fifty years just died. Your father has died. Roger—" "She'll get soaked," Reverend Jarvis interjected, and that was the final word, apparently. Belle would stay in the limo. Phillip didn't argue. He wasn't sure of what he wanted. I returned to the limo. Belle inspected me disapprovingly. My coat was damp. "You've probably caught a cold," she told me. There was a streak of lightning, then thunder. For a second I thought I was trapped in an old Walt Disney movie—the castle against a purple sky, the crackling lightning in the sky, the dungeon deep under the castle with the good guy held prisoner in ankle irons.

Phil and the driver returned. The driver turned on the engine. I thought we were heading closer to the grave site, but we made a U-turn and our limo led the caravan of cars out through the wrought iron gates of the cemetery. "The rain might let up in ten or fifteen minutes," I whispered to Phil; "ask Mom if she wants to wait." He didn't want to ask his mother, so I said, "Mom, do you want to stay here and have the burial? Maybe we should wait ten or fifte minutes. The rain will probably let up and we can go through with the service." I glanced at Phil who was expressionless. Belle shrugged. Enid didn't say anything. The children were silent. The only sound in the limo was the decisive smacking of the windshield wipers. For a few moments I felt comforted by that rhythmic beat until I glanced at Matina and Eric; their expressions were identical, as if they were watching their own scary film. I tried to imagine what they were seeing: their grandfather sliding down, down that deep chute, alone. Or something else? I didn't want to believe they were in that much pain. I wanted Belle or Enid or someone to touch them, comfort them, make them happy again, but no one did and they were out of my reach.

At Belle's apartment the crowd of family and friends, the table arranged with platters of cold cuts and salads, the almost partylike atmosphere soothed me and stopped my nasty script writing. I like tribal gatherings, of which I've had all too few in my own family, even though there was the early promise—at Grandma Doland's cavernous apartment on Sunday afternoons when I was very young. The whole family gathered. Aunt Birdie yakking on and on about nothing. Uncle Lionel, beautifully dressed. Do these memories of the family as tribe leave indelible impressions on us—the imprint of life as it *should* be lived?

Matina and I tried to find a way to make ourselves useful while Eric was taking people's orders for drinks. Justin, Phillip's good-looking cousin, was bartending. I waved at him but didn't go over. Matina and I found a couple of fruit baskets to unpack, and we arranged apples and pears and grapes in a cut-glass bowl. Neither of us spoke, but we rolled our eyes when we heard Belle's voice above the others saying yet again, "I've lost my best friend." She was sitting on the couch flanked by her two children, determined not to take any comfort in them. I fixed a plate of food for her and brought it over and she accepted it without looking at me or thanking me. I offered to fix plates for Phillip and Enid, too. Enid nodded but Phil wanted to get up and stretch his legs.

As he moved away from Belle, Uncle Gordie and a couple of other men gathered around him. It was the business they wanted to talk about with Phillip. I think it was the business they wanted to eulogize: a strong healthy business that had grown with the times. *Grown with the times*, that was the important phrase. The business was now in Phillip's hands, the third generation of Stedmans, over seventy-five years of fine wallpapers. The first generation of Stedmans manufactured wallpapers, and the recent Stedmans imported them from Japan and Italy. Phillip looked shaky. "I wonder if we should go ahead and open the Chicago showroom? Or maybe we should postpone those plans for a while." Uncle Gordie put his hand on Phil's back. "Phil, go ahead with them."

Glancing at Uncle Gordie, his drooping white mustache, his ruddy complexion, I remembered what Roger had once told me about his brother-in-law, Gordie—that he'd "pissed away" his wife's money on bum investments in New Mexico real estate and Oklahoma oil. I chuckled thinking how ugly Roger could be. And yet a spiky flame of love made me calm. He thought I was a smart, sexy woman, and I have to admit, I loved him for thinking that.

My spirits picked up, buoyed by the hum of voices in the ample living room with its cream-colored rug and one long, wallpapered wall, a floral pattern that Roger had said was a copy of a wallpaper from the Plaza Hotel circa 1900. He had been proud of his line of famous wallpapers, the old authentic ones that he occasionally donated to historic restorations.

I spotted Justin at the far end of the room, through a haze of cigarette smoke and at a distance from the center of chatter. Over the course of fifteen years at these occasional family gatherings we had a little flirtatious ritual that involved calling each other "cuz," essentially silly and vacuous, although each of us knew we found the other attractive. It was all very proper and balanced until he divorced his wife Bugsie a couple of years ago. Then at his parents' forty-fifth anniversary party last year we avoided each other for the first half of the party—but the regret on both sides was palpable. If you ask me how I knew that, all I can say is that I did. And maybe Roger did, too. At one point he actually encouraged me to dance with Justin—why would Roger do that?— but dance we did. After two minutes into the "Anniversary Waltz," Justin and I veered off to a phone booth in an empty hallway and molded ourselves against each other, and kissed, and then panicked that someone would see us. We stayed that way, and for a few minutes I didn't care whether anyone saw us. In that tiny interval of time, he slid his hand down the front of my dress and touched my breast. Now as I was about to approach Justin, Phillip signaled me into the den. I could tell by his expression that he wanted me to do something that would be difficult for me to do. Sometimes he wanted me to make what I'd call a "unilateral sacrifice." Phillip wanted me to be dutiful for the both of us. He wanted me to go the extra mile, while he retreated or hid, or simply vanished.

What he had in mind was for me to offer to stay with Belle and Enid tonight so that Enid wouldn't feel saddled with all the responsibility. "It may be a rough night for Mom," he said. He would take Eric and Matina home and see that they got to school in the morning and tie up some problems at the office. Then he'd come back to Huntstown tomorrow and we could drive home together in the evening. His idea seemed reasonable, sweet, thoughtful. I agreed—but in my mind I had one condition: that Belle express some desire for me to stay. If it made no difference to her, then I would back out of my offer. I needed one tiny sign that I could be of some comfort.

I didn't tell Phil about my one condition, but we lingered alone in the den for a moment or two. "I'll ask her," I repeated. He nodded, pleased; he didn't look at me. He spoke into the room, in the direction of the window, not me. "We should have stayed at the cemetery and buried Dad," he whispered. "The rain wasn't that bad." He was handing me a sharp little knife and it was up to me not to use it.

I squeezed onto the couch next to Belle, who was sitting with Enid and other relatives. I asked how she was doing, whether she had been able to eat anything? Could I get her a cup of tea? No, she was fine. Then I asked, "Mom, what if I stay here with you and Enid tonight?" She stared at me as if I were speaking a foreign language. "Why?" she asked. "To keep you and Enid company tonight." "If you want to," she said.

I felt trapped, or more accurately that I had swum willingly into a fishnet, one of those invisible nylon filament fishnets. Then I surprised myself. I said, "I guess I would rather go home and sleep in my own bed." "Well no one's stopping you," Belle said. "You've been very helpful through all this. So have the children."

It was as easy as that.

·   ·   ·

In the car in the dark heading toward Manhattan, Eric said, "People really boozed it up today, Dad. We finished off Grandpa Roger's Scotch, his Canadian Club, and half a bottle of Tanqueray gin. I know 'cause I was helping make drinks with Justin."

"Grandpa wouldn't have minded," Phillip said.

"He liked a party," I said, picturing Roger moving slyly among family and friends, touching the women, letting his hands rove a little too close to breast and ass. I remembered how, off to one side, he had spied on me dancing with Justin.

"In a way it *was* like a party," Matina said, but Phillip, who was morose, disagreed. Matina persisted. "I guess a funeral has to be like a party," she mused. "I mean, we're alive. The rest of us go on living. We can't stop; there's no choice. And we're happy about it." The idea was brand-new to her, startling. How many people did she know who had died? One or two? She leaned forward toward her father. "And Grandpa had a good life, don't you think, Dad?"

"Definitely," Phillip replied. "He worked hard and he was happy when business was good."

"But no one really cried during the service," Eric said. "Grandma Belle didn't. I didn't, no one did."

"Will you remember your grandfather?" Phillip asked, and it was Eric, not Matina, who answered, "Always," and Phillip, pleased, quickly wanted to shape those memories. "Your grandfather was a friendly man, always had a warm greeting for everyone. You should have seen him on the train in the mornings." Before he could describe Roger's early morning cheer on the commuter train, I asked him if his father had been friendly to *him*. It wasn't a wise question, I realized too late. I was pushing him for shading, for qualification. For my take on the truth. Pushing too soon, too much.

For a while no one spoke. I was grateful for the speed we were traveling at and for the great, glittering jewel box of a city we were heading toward. I was grateful I wasn't spending the night with Belle and Enid, although I had the feeling that Phillip was furious at me for not.

Matina, who'd been amazingly quiet for a long time, had a question. Her body began to bristle with energy and small stretching motions. Matina was born asking questions; even her baby burps, it had seemed to us, came out sounding like questions. "I didn't understand why we didn't get out of the limo and see Grandpa get buried," she asked. "Is that usual? It didn't seem right."

I prayed for restraint. I said to myself, *Harriet, keep your goddamn mouth shut.*

"It would have been too painful for Grandma," Phillip said. "She might have broken down, and besides, it was going to pour. We would have all gotten soaked."

Matina didn't say anything and neither did I. Eric announced the time: 9:51. He wanted to know whether he had to go to school in the morning. Phil and I answered together. I said *No*, Phillip said *Yes*. "I want to go," Matina stated. "You would," Eric replied. "We'll give you the official answer later," I told Eric, who belabored the point by saying he'd be too tired in the morning to get to school on time.

"Poor Grandma," Eric said, "she's lost her best friend." And it was only when Eric said those words that I could feel the sorrowful truth of them. "Yes," I said, "Roger was Belle's best friend." I no longer could belittle that fact. But when I stopped making fun of Belle, a staticky wave of anxiety tremored through me and I wanted to open my mouth wide and roar like a lion.

•   •   •

The family flew apart the moment we entered the apartment. The children disappeared, and soon two stereos were screaming out reggae and rock, not an altogether unpleasant combination. Phillip changed out of his suit and headed for the kitchen. I heard the clink of glasses being lined up in the cabinet and knew he was emptying the dishwasher. Often when he was upset about something he would work in the kitchen or clean things that I overlooked like the top of the refrigerator or the wall behind the stove. Of all the possible nervous habits, it was a useful one, I have to admit. I turned on a single lamp and settled into an armchair in the living room and sorted through my mail. The room was dim and lifeless. Phillip was in the kitchen, the children in their separate rooms. A wave of fear came over me, a thick strap tightening and tightening around my ribs. The strap pulled tighter. I could scarcely breathe. It was breaking me in half. A few seconds later I was aware that music was coming only from Eric's room; also voices, the scraping of furniture.

I cracked open Eric's door and saw him dancing with Matina in the area between the bunkbed and bookshelves. The desk chair had been stacked on top of the desk and the desk pushed flush with the wall and the small rug heaped in the corner. They spotted me, but continued moving to Jimmy Cliff's "You Can Get It If You Really Want." Eric's bare feet caressed the floor, patted it. Even his toes seemed alert. As I watched him I began to breathe. His dancing fascinated me, the dignity of it. He had wrapped a red sash around his waist. I noticed how steadily he held his head. For a second he reminded me of one of those West Point cadets, the kind you used to see in posters, with incredible posture and blue-eyed fortitude and optimism. He saw the best in everyone. The other part, what wasn't the best, didn't interest him. Matina and he moved through the next song, aware of each other but not overly so.

When the next song began, Eric said, "Ma, c'mon, dance with us," and Matina echoed her brother's invitation. At first I refused but they were insistent. "Please, Ma," Matina said, "please dance with us." There was a seriousness to her tone that made me submit. I joined them, and they seemed relieved. My body was stiff at first. I still had pain in my middle.

We danced and danced; the calves of my legs hurt but I began to breathe. I knew that if I could just keep going at some point the music would find me and I'd grow lighter. I don't think any of us could have stopped even if we'd wanted to, and we didn't want to. The small area between the bed and the shelves seemed ample: our movements weren't wild. Matina and Eric danced around me and I, around them. Now and again we touched each other, held hands.

During the next song I spotted Phillip in the doorway in his undershirt. I liked seeing his bare shoulders and his arms and his throat, his skin honey-colored and warm-looking even in November. I waved him in but I didn't stop dancing. I danced harder. As he stood there watching us, the color drained from his face, and his eyes turned to slits, and his disapproval seemed cold and righteous, as though he knew for certain that the dead don't like dancing. But I knew he was absolutely wrong about that. He remained in the doorway, and Eric said, "Join us, Dad, please," but Phillip blinked and shook his head, no. He shook his head and disappeared. He always knew what he didn't want to do. *He was so god-*

damn confident about what he didn't want to do. I gazed at the empty doorway, that hard-edged rectangle of space, and my voice echoed silently, *good-bye, good-bye.* . . .

The three of us kept on, our bodies melting and elongating like vertical accordions. Matina glanced at me as if she knew that her parents' marriage was moments away from ending. As if she'd known it all day. For the first time in her life there were no questions, no perfect shining questions bubbling up over and around her. We kept on dancing through the sound of a glass crashing to the floor, and then another, and then another. The children pretended not to hear, or maybe they didn't. I heard the glasses crashing and shattering on the floor, but I couldn't stop dancing. Something was started . . . It had taken so many years. So many years. And now we were there. Neither Eric nor Matina looked at me. My legs ached, but I kept on moving.

Charity Work

My father, carrying me out into the surf, told me that all life comes from the sea, that our blood itself is made of salt water. My mother said, "Harriet, slip out of your bathing suit and see how soft the water feels on your body." My father's chest was smooth and sunburned pink. His arms had freckles and there was a bulge in his tight shiny swimming trunks. I saw my mother's breasts, even the points of her nipples, when she leaned over to help me out of my bathing suit. The ocean turned us into bodies: its buoyancy, I think, or maybe that small jump you have to take in order to ride up and up and up over a wave. The sharpest memories of my father occurred within one short period of time—the summer we rented the cottage at Seaview, a sleepy, makeshift summer town on the Jersey Shore.

My parents rented a cottage in Seaview the summer I was eight. We had never done that before, and never would again. Not only my family of three in our white cottage, but Grandma Doland and Aunt Mary and Aunt Birdie, who was my father's retarded sister, in their mint green cottage. Uncle Lionel Doland, my lawyer uncle, and his pretty wife and their twin babies in another cottage, a lemon-colored one. We made up a kind of Doland family "estate" although we were just renting small cottages. We were far from being rich. My father was a bus driver in Newark.

That summer he was able to get occasional three-day weekends and a two-week vacation and I saw more of him than I ever had in my life. He liked to swim in the late afternoon when the water was rough and green and the waves high. He carried me into the surf and jumped the waves and wore a playful expression on his face, an expression I associate now with dolphins—beautiful, endangered dolphins. I put my arms around his neck and my cheek against his, and once I licked his cheek and tasted the salt of the sea, and he laughed at me and didn't seem to mind. After that, all summer, whenever he took me out into the ocean, I did that—I licked his rough, sunburned cheek and tasted the salt, and he laughed. It was the first time he didn't mind my acting silly.

I was happy to be living in a cottage at the beach close to my father's relatives, whom I saw only on occasional Sundays and holidays in their dark cavernous apartment in New York City on Amsterdam Avenue and Eighty-second Street—before Amsterdam Avenue was part of creeping chic. I loved going to that apartment. Those dark rooms and windowless hallways held secrets, unhappy stories, mysteries, disappearances—things that didn't go on in our sunny four-room apartment in Enfield, New Jersey. How did Birdie get her hunchback?—or what had Aunt Mary's husband done that was so bad?—or what had happened to Grandpa Doland? My heart beat fast when I walked into the lobby of that building. The walls of the lobby were made of marble, swirly and streaked, pink and liver brown, with blue veins. I imagined I was going *inside* of a body.

At Seaview my mother, whose own mother had died when she was eleven, seemed to relish running across the street to see whether Grandma needed something from the market, or bringing her a bowl of egg salad for lunch, or sitting out on the screened-in porch of Grandma's cottage talking, although I never thought Grandma was much of a talker. Birdie was the talker. Birdie talked on and on about the same things over and over again, and Grandma let her. My mother admired Grandma for never complaining about Birdie, whose mind would stay like a six-year-old's for the rest of her life. My mother found endless proof that Grandma was a pillar of patience and generosity. The real proof, however, was the fact that Grandma did charity work: she visited old people at St. Agnes' Hospital downtown. My mother would often say that she wanted to be a volunteer at a hospital like Grandma Doland, but my mother never seemed to find the right hospital.

"Sweetheart, don't feel obliged to do charity work just because my mother does," I heard my father tell my mother after supper one night during the previous winter. "I'm not saying Mother isn't a wonderful person, but you're wonderful, too, Rosalie." He touched my mother's cheek with his fingers and told her that she had the loveliest blue eyes in the world. "I honestly want to volunteer," my mother said, "if only I could find a hospital where the patients aren't so sick and where the nurses are nice." "Well if you do," my father muttered, "don't carry it too far." His tone took on an unfamiliar gruffness, and he rose from his chair and wandered over to the window and stared out into the night. I thought I heard him whisper, "Charity begins at home," but maybe I made that up. He kept his face close to the windowpane and his breath steamed it up.

I have to admit that at Seaview my mother didn't only pay attention to Grandma Doland. She spent time with me. She loved the beach and took me swimming in the morning before breakfast when the ocean was calm. First we walked along the water's edge where the waves broke quietly, with scarcely any foam; bubbles— lazy, sweet bubbles. I thought I heard my mother humming. The beach was deserted except for a fisherman or two. Seaweed, dead fish, old pieces of tarry wood, seagull feathers, shells, crab claws. The silvery blue fish smelled rotten; they stank. I found a stick and poked at them.

In the water my mother said, "Honey, slip out of your bathing suit and feel the water on your body." I held my legs together and wiggled from side to side like a mermaid. For a moment or two I floated, head up, staring at the sky, then head down, turning over and over. I pretended I was swimming, but I let my hands touch bottom and hoped my mother would be fooled. "You're beginning to swim," she said, smiling.

After our early morning dips we went back to our cottage and had breakfast at a faded red Formica table with silver legs in front of a window that faced the street. Outside there were blue hydrangeas and bushes with tiny hard, red berries. Over coffee my mother would read the *Seaview Daily Gazette*, which was delivered to the door by a newsboy.

One morning after she finished reading the paper, she said, "Harriet dear, bring this newspaper over to Grandma's; she might enjoy reading it."

I found Grandma on the porch. She didn't notice me at first. She was standing over Birdie, combing her short straight hair with sharp slaps of the comb. Then, from what I could see, she yanked Birdie's hair together and fastened it on the side with a barrette.

Birdie yelled "Ouch" and Grandma snapped, "Oh, be quiet!" When Grandma saw me, she brightened. I was wearing my red shorts and a red-striped polo shirt. I handed her the newspaper and told her it was from my mother. She said, "How thoughtful of her!" A few seconds later she said, "I have an idea, Harriet. In the mornings after your mother finishes reading the paper, bring it over to me and I'll pay you ten cents. That way you'll have your first job." As I was leaving I heard her murmur, "May God bless you."

I liked the idea of earning money. There was a small wiry Mickey Mouse doll in the window of the candy shop down on Main Street that I had admired and which my mother wouldn't buy me because I had "enough dolls." I was an only child and she worried about spoiling me. Now I realized that if I saved my money I could buy it for myself. I loved that Mickey Mouse already, his spindly black legs, his big clumsy feet, his perfectly rounded mouse ears, the black plum of a nose: something so lovable and spunky and sad about him.

The idea of a job made me feel important and I ran back to our cottage and told my mother about it.

"Your first job!" she exclaimed. "I hope you said 'thank you.'" There was a trace of nervousness in her voice as though this new job might be a test for both of us. "We'll have to figure out where you can save your money." She searched in her dresser drawer and found a red zipper change purse and handed it to me.

Over the next couple of weeks I brought Grandma the paper and she showed me how to play tic-tac-toe. Away from her dark apartment on Amsterdam Avenue she wasn't as serious; and yet still, she didn't seem to breathe. She never opened her mouth, never yawned, never laughed. Her words came out of the inside of her like a ventriloquist's.

The dimes piled up in my red change purse. My mother was proud of me. "Well, sweetie, you've saved a lot of money," she told me in the middle of August. Every so often, usually when my father was with us, we went for a walk on Main Street and I would steer them past the candy store where little Mickey was in the window. One day I overheard my father say, "Rosalie, let's get her the Mickey Mouse doll," but my mother shot him a look, a serious look. Instead my father bought me a bag of assorted caramels.

About a week later, as my mother fluffed out and brushed my hair, she said, "I have an idea for what you can do with your earnings."

"I already know! I'm going to buy the Mickey Mouse doll." I was very confident.

My mother continued to brush my hair. "Harriet honey, you have a million dolls at home. Why don't we take your money and I'll add to it, and we'll treat the children at St. Vincent's Hospital to ice cream."

I knew that it made more sense to point out that the children in the hospital probably had plenty of ice cream than to say how much I wanted the Mickey Mouse doll. You weren't supposed to want anything—that's what I was beginning to learn. The less you wanted and the more you gave away, the more wonderful you were.

"You're a lucky kid," my mother said.

"How come I'm so lucky?" I asked, knowing it was a question I wasn't supposed to ask.

She searched for an answer, her hand on top of her head. The question startled her. "You have a mother," she answered, her tone slightly harsh; then a few seconds later she added, "and a father."

On the next Thursday my mother and I took a bus to St. Vincent's Hospital in the next town, about fifteen minutes away. St. Vincent's had a children's ward and was run by nuns. They wore eyeglasses with steel frames. They carried Bibles and wore crosses around their necks and rosaries dangled from their apron pockets, or from their hands, from everywhere. I was never raised as a Catholic, although Grandma Doland, I'm sure, would have liked it. My father didn't care for religion.

The children's ward was boiling hot. A nun in white led my mother and me into a large room with enormous, tightly shut windows and a row of beds on each side. The beds were like cribs. I forced myself to look at the children, most of whom had contraptions on their bodies: braces, casts, pulleys with weights, harnesses. One tiny girl was sitting in a tiny wooden wheelchair next to her bed while a nun in black was making her bed without ever looking at her. She reminded me of Birdie, but smaller. I noticed the neatness of the beds and the awful silence and the heat of the room, and I stood closer to my mother.

Presently a cart with dishes and ice cream was wheeled into the center of the room by a nun in white. She scooped the ice cream, and my mother signaled me to go over to Sister so that I could take the saucers of ice cream around to the children. Everything about that room frightened me. If I breathed in too deeply I was afraid I would smell the rotting fish on the beach. In the silence I thought I could hear screams.

I brought a boy his ice cream. He said, "Hello, my name is Anthony. What's your name?"

"Harriet."

"How old are you?"

"Just eight."

"When's your birthday?"

"May."

"What's your name?"

"Harriet."

Again he asked me how old I was. I searched the room for my mother who was talking to the sister in white, next to the cart. Anthony was like a record with a scratch on it and I was the needle caught in the scratch. "Excuse me," I said to Anthony, "I have to bring ice cream to the other children."

A small boy, his feet gripped to a bar with weights on the end, called out to me. He had a rash on the inside of his arms. I handed him a bowl of ice cream. "Do you got any bubble gum?" he asked. I shook my head. "Do me a favor, girlie. Give these baseball cards to Lenny. He's the kid with the cast on his leg." The boy pointed to a black boy at the far end of the ward. The cards were sticky and when I walked across the room everybody stared at me. I gave the cards to Lenny. I noticed how his dark brown toes stuck out of the chalky whiteness of his cast. I pictured myself running errands forever and ever between the boy with the rash on his arms and the boy with the cast on his leg.

I brought an older girl her ice cream. She was a teenager, I think. A plaster cast covered her entire body and a bad smell steamed up out of the cast. For a second I thought I smelled b.m. Only her face and her hair, which was thick and red, stuck out of the cast. The girl asked me how old I was, and while I told her, she gobbled down her ice cream. "See if you can get me more ice cream, honey," the girl said.

The children seemed like prisoners of their beds, and I was a prisoner of them all. And my mother sat on a chair far away on the other side of the room, talking to the nun in white, not looking at me. I tried to catch her eye but couldn't. My mother was wearing a blue dress with a million tiny white daisies, white earrings, a white bead necklace. She had on high heels. I remember thinking that she looked prettier than I had ever seen her look. I had the feeling that she was happy. She was finally doing charity work.

When I finished giving out the ice cream, the nun made a speech thanking me for giving a treat to sick children with the money I earned from delivering newspapers. I hid myself behind my mother, out of view of the children. I wished I had refused to serve the ice cream. My mother should have served it; after all, it was *her* idea.

On the way back to Seaview, my mother bought ice-cream cones at a drugstore lunch counter, one for me and one for herself. As we left the drugstore, she said, "The nun and I had an interesting talk. She said that many of the children never have visitors—no one to talk to, no gifts, no treats. Week after week—no visitors." I slowed my pace. I didn't want to hear another word about sick children. "Walk a little faster, Harriet," my mother urged. I tried to walk as slowly as I could.

The next morning when I brought the newspaper over to Grandma Doland, she said, "I hear you went to St. Vincent's yesterday. May the Blessed Mother smile on you." She touched her fingers to my cheek and leaned toward me, but didn't smile. She wasn't a smiling grandma.

I missed my Mickey Mouse.

"Out of sorts?" Grandma said. "I won't keep you," and she handed me fifty cents—two quarters. "A bonus for being such a good girl."

The money was useless, I thought as I went back to our cottage where my mother was packing a picnic lunch for the beach. I would never get the Mickey Mouse doll.

"What did grandma say about the hospital?" my mother asked me.

"Nothing," I replied, "but she gave me fifty cents."

"Didn't Grandma Doland *say* anything?" my mother asked again; "I would have thought she would have been so proud of you."

"Nope," I said, and handed my mother the fifty cents. "Here, give the money to kids who need it."

My mother looked sad. "Are you sure Grandma didn't say anything?" she asked again, refusing to take the two quarters and turning back to the picnic lunch. When her back was turned, I took the two quarters and hurled them out the window into the blue hydrangeas. I promised myself I would never go swimming with her again before breakfast, and I didn't.

In spite of the hospital and not getting the Mickey Mouse doll, it was a lovely summer. I helped take care of Uncle Lionel and Aunt Sue's baby twins, and Aunt Sue gave me one of her flowered silk scarves as a present. Once she and Uncle Lionel took me to an amusement park. "The child doesn't need to see freaks," my grandmother said to Uncle Lionel before we left. "It's okay, Mother," Uncle Lionel told her. "Don't worry. She'll be fine." He was firm with Grandma. I've already seen a freak, I wanted to say—Aunt Birdie; her hump seemed enormous to me, her head like a turtle's head.

Every Sunday afternoon all of us brought casseroles and salads over to Uncle Lionel and Aunt Sue's house—because theirs was the biggest cottage and faced the ocean—and had dinner on their screened-in porch. My father brought out beers and passed them around, and sat and drank and smoked and watched. At those times Aunt Birdie would sit herself next to my father and start yakking. Birdie, I noticed, didn't yak as much when Uncle Lionel was around. Uncle Lionel was more jovial than my father, but once in a while I heard him scold Birdie. "Okay, okay! Enough!" when she was talking too much. Once I heard him tell her to shut the hell up, she was driving him nuts. My father never would have said anything like that. Instead he listened and got a faraway look in his eyes. At those times his face seemed to turn white and he'd light up a cigarette and forget to flick the ash. He seemed to go into deep freeze until the cigarette stub burnt his fingers and then he'd toss it to the concrete floor and stomp on it.

My mother noticed that white, mean, deep-freeze look on my father's face and I overheard her ask him what was wrong. He answered in a voice that scared me: "I can't stand listening to Birdie go on and on. It's like I came to a line in myself and I can't go over it. So many years of her yakking . . ."

But more and more it seemed that my mother went out of her way to pay attention to Birdie, to have long conversations with her, to look at the picture puzzle she was working on and ask her questions about it. I began to think that my mother paid more attention to Birdie than to me. Once she bought a new cotton dress for Birdie. White with purple swans. The dress was too long, and my mother had to sew up the hem, and it took her hours to do. She did the sewing over at Grandma's cottage, one evening on the porch. Birdie was yakking on and on about a new picture puzzle, and my mother was complimenting her on being able to do a thousand-piece puzzle. Suddenly my father stood up and slammed out the door and headed toward the beach. I knew he went for a walk on the beach because when he came back he took off his shoes and emptied a pile of sand from each shoe right onto the floor of the porch. Birdie was still yakking to my mother.

A couple of days later my mother bought Birdie white earrings—"summer jewelry" she called it. "Why shouldn't Birdie have some summer jewelry like Aunt Mary or Aunt Sue?" she said to me in the store. Uncle Lionel was supposedly the big spender in the family, but he didn't spend money on Birdie. My mother did. One evening I overheard my father tell my mother that he knew for a fact that Birdie had a drawerful of summer jewelry and that she shouldn't feel obliged to pay so much attention to her. "Don't carry this thing too far, Rosalie," he warned. "You'll end up spending every minute of your life and all your money on Babette." He called Aunt Birdie by her real name, and I thought he sounded angry. "We have to lighten your mother's burden," my mother replied. "Let Lionel be the one to lighten my mother's burden," my father whispered, lighting a cigarette.

On August 31 we left Seaview, went back to Enfield, and I started third grade. All three of us talked about the good summer the family had had together and how nice it was to have a big family. But in December, a week after Thanksgiving, my father disappeared—and in the next two years we heard from him only once, and he never came back to live with my mother or me again. He moved to Oregon. I've often thought about that summer and tried to figure out whether there were any clues as to why he left. My mother said that the ocean made him restless. Maybe. But once in a while I believed it was because of me, because I was selfish, because I didn't want to do charity work.

During Christmas season my mother was busy consoling Grandma Doland. Sometimes I worried that my mother had fallen in love with Grandma Doland. I wasn't sure. All I knew was that waves were pouring over me and I was jumbled up in them, drowning in them and under them. I was suffocating and dying. No one was holding me tight. And four or five months later when I came up for air, I found myself living in the dark cavelike apartment on Eighty-second Street and Amsterdam Avenue—with Grandma Doland, Aunt Mary, Birdie, and my mother. I was inside the body. I was inside the body, but all I could taste was dust.

Dancing with Time

S now frightens me: its relentlessness; its power to cover up all that's familiar. I leaned my chin against the back of the couch and watched the feathery dots smash against the window. It was the last day of the year. Matina and her friend were in the kitchen making miniature foods from homemade Play-Doh; Eric, who was napping, would wake up soon. Outside on a maple tree a blue jay jittered from branch to branch. I resented its vigor. Less than a mile away my friend Paul Miner was dying.

Eight months ago when Paul was healthy, seemingly healthy, I'd stood in his pottery studio with stacks of cups and bowls waiting to be fired, and tried to coax him into action. For weeks he'd been talking about his "sloth." I thought he was joking. Sloth—his big word. "I'm falling into total *sloth*, Harriet."

"Your sloth could pass for somebody else's high gear," I said.

"I have no spark," he insisted.

I looked at him—fit as a fiddle. He was a good-looking man, a full head of chestnut brown hair, smoky gray eyes in a narrow face, slim and agile, young for his forty-seven years. I was only thirty. "Here's what I think you should do," I said. "First see a doctor and have a thorough checkup, and if he can't find anything wrong with you, get yourself a good shrink."

How full of good advice I'd been! How young! Paul, however, took my advice, and he didn't need the shrink.

The first time Phillip and I met Paul was two years earlier, before Eric was born, on the frozen pond behind the Huntstown Golf Club when we were trying to teach Matina to ice-skate. "Yoo-hoo," he'd called, "I want to meet you." He pretended to skate over to us, hands clasped behind his back, sliding along, no ice skates on his feet, just rubber-soled boots. He knelt in front of Matina and tightened the laces on her skates. His face tilted up toward hers, and he spoke a few words to her in a teasing, sweet way. I noticed his red, chapped hands, and only later did it dawn on me why they were red—the hands of a potter, in and out of water. Soon he was pulling Matina away from us. She was more confident with him than with us.

When he came back with her a few minutes later, he offered to do figure eights for us. In a fitted black jacket and a boxy Russian-style black Persian lamb hat, he turned into a dark cutout figure against the silver ice. His movements took on the stylized quality of karate or tai chi. Then he spread his arms and turned into a hawk gliding on an air current. I loved watching him, although I noticed that Phillip turned away and let his eyes rest on the soft breasty hills of the golf course.

We went to the Minerses' for hot chocolate and stayed for dinner. Vicki, his wife, was one of those women who knew how to cook the basics, like mashed potatoes or pot roast or buttermilk biscuits, so that they're more delicious than gourmet food. She served us dinner in Paul's earthenware bowls, on platters and plates glazed blue-green or a mustardy ochre. Paul told us that Vicki was the manager of a small employment agency. She was the family's main financial support while he had run through a succession of jobs, none of which was right for him until about five years ago when he discovered pottery in an evening ceramics class at the high school.

"Huntstown High?" Phillip asked, explaining that he had taken ceramics in that same remarkably well-equipped pottery when he was sixteen.

"Any time you feel like using my wheel, feel free," Paul said.

Vicki was hospitable, but there was a quality of exhaustion about her, or maybe it was fear. Paul was the one with warmth. I was growing aware of how couples gravitate toward complementarity so that one person's strength crowds out the other's capacity for that strength altogether. Paul was loving and open; Vicki, reserved. We stayed late and ended up carrying Matina home sleeping.

Matina and her friend were still turning out an assortment of Play-Doh foods when Phillip called from Penn Station. Because of the sleet and snow the trains were running late. He and his dad might be an hour late. Phil worked for his father in his wholesale wallpaper company in Manhattan. "Please call Mom and tell her," Phillip said, and I did. "I thought that might be the case," his mother, Belle, said, "not so much because of the snow but because of the holiday." She didn't sound concerned, whereas I suddenly saw the railroad tracks encased in ice.

Matina and Jody were getting bored. "Make a chicken for me, Mama," Matina commanded. I tried, squeezing the bit of Play-Doh into a chickeny shape without much success, then offered to make a heaping bowl of spaghetti. I took the garlic press and squeezed a lump of dough through it and piled the thin, minute strands on a flat plate formed from a coin-sized piece of dough. After a while I tackled the chicken again. I was an experienced nursery school teacher, so I was good at dreaming up activities.

There were a couple of whimpers from Eric's room, then quiet again. When I glanced out the kitchen window I could see the snow burying the trees and the bushes and the rooftops on the next street. White blended with white. There were no landmarks, no streets, no boundaries between anything. I'd invited some friends over for New Year's Eve, including Paul and Vicki, and I wondered whether anybody would come. Half the friends we had were splitting up. It was snowing hard. Phillip wasn't home yet. My friend Paul was dying.

From the open shelves I took down ceramic mugs for hot mulled cider. I had more than a dozen. Paul had made them and brought them over one or two at a time whenever he came to visit. His face had a sort of boyish expression. *Hey, can you believe what I've been able to make from a lump of clay!* He'd pull mugs out of the deep pockets of his coat the way a magician pulls scarves out of his sleeves. Then he'd loop his fingers into the handles of the mugs and let them dangle so that we could see the different glazes and surfaces. They would sway dangerously close to each other. Ceramics was magic to him: not just the technology of it, but how he'd become a person with gifts for everyone. At his studio I learned to be careful not to admire anything because if I did, it would turn up on my doorstep the next day.

The phone rang. Margot Kelman, her voice reedy and distant. If it didn't stop snowing they wouldn't be able to make it. "Please try," I begged. "Paul and Vicki are coming. Please . . ." "Would you mind if I came without Jay?" Margot asked. "Of course not," I said and meant it. "Try to join us, Margot." I didn't want Paul and Vicki to be our only guests. In my mind's eye I could see Paul's bony fingers circling one of his own mugs. I could see him sneak a look at his watch to see whether it was time to slug down another painkiller.

It was Phillip on the phone when it rang next. I was holding Eric, that delicious bundle of baby with an easy-to-please disposition. Phillip was at the supermarket. Did we need anything? Milk? Bread? There might be a blizzard.

"I can't think of anything we need," I said. "Come home, drive carefully." I knew that the roads were slick. "Phil, I feel so sad. . . ."

"Tell me about it when I get home," he said, and I knew that he believed that at the bottom of my sadness was a complaint about him, and often that was unfortunately the case. I had my dissatisfactions: with Huntstown, with his parents whom I loved less and less, with him because I wanted him to think I was amazing and I don't think he did. And of course I wasn't amazing. It's not easy at thirty to admit that you're dissatisfied with yourself. I was reading books to Matina about extraordinary women — Madame Curie and Florence Nightingale and Amelia Earhart and Maria Mitchell, "girl astronomer" — and I wanted a mission, a cause, a discovery to make. "Drive slowly, Phillip," I said again, and at that point Matina asked me to help Jody and herself into snowsuits.

Outside it was no longer a suburb of look-alike houses. It was a land of no houses, of no people. The future was buried in snowdrifts. I didn't hear Jody's father pull into the driveway, and there he was! — full of New Year's cheer, snowflakes sticking to his dark wool hat, melting on his cheeks and nose. I had noticed him at parent-teacher meetings at Matina's school. He moved with a kind of built-in bounce, like a basketball player walking the ball down the court, his energy centered in his Jockey shorts. He swooped down and lifted up his daughter and inspected the miniature foods she'd made. He knew right away that his daughter hadn't made the chicken. Jody pointed to me. Smiling appreciatively, he kissed my cheek with his wet face against mine, and I wanted to cling to him and not let go. He thanked me for taking Jody for the afternoon and wished us all a Happy New Year and left.

When Phillip chugged home a few minutes later I felt more in the New Year's Eve spirit of things, and yet at the same time I was more certain that no one was going to show up for this party, especially not Paul and Vicki. But everyone *except* Paul and Vicki called to cancel, and then a short while later Vicki called—not to cancel, but to see if we could drive them home later if they walked over to our house. "It won't be too tiring for Paul to walk?" "He wants to," Vicki said. I could hear her exhaustion. "Okay, we'll be waiting for you." I tried to sound cheerful.

Matina, who had every intention of staying up till midnight, said, "I thought Uncle Paul was sick. How can he walk here? What is cancer anyway?" She kept trying to make sense out of our quasi-scientific explanations and I wished that Phillip hadn't stimulated her and used the expression, "runaway cells." In a week or two she'd be asking me whether *her* cells would run away. But Phillip didn't like glossing over solid facts.

We put Matina and Eric to bed, promising to wake Matina up when the new year arrived.

"Sweetheart, go to sleep now," I said, wanting Matina to fall asleep before she realized that any one of us could get cancer— from smoking or not. "Shhh . . ." I murmured softly, "go to sleep." I sat on the edge of her bed and rubbed her back for about ten minutes and then kissed her thick, curly hair, which was warm and sweet smelling. I tiptoed out of her room knowing perfectly well that she wasn't asleep.

Downstairs Phillip crouched in front of the fire, feeding the sluggish flames twigs and strips of newspaper. "I'm afraid to see Paul standing in the doorway," he said almost angrily, and he seemed angry with *me*—for making a friend who would die. "I wish the Kelmans were coming or the Robertses," Phillip went on. "We need more people."

Phillip's fear acted as a start-up switch for my courage. It was that complementarity thing; I grew confident, expansive, even poetic, as Phillip shrank from the idea of being with Paul. I became sensitive and brave and compassionate. I went so far as to imagine giving Paul some testimony of my love. Paul, my dear friend. He'd been particularly kind to me, something I didn't expect from men, or from anyone for that matter. He'd helped me out once when I was sick and feverish and couldn't deal with Matina; he'd taken her out with him for an entire afternoon so that I could sleep. I had called Phillip and asked him to come home but he absolutely couldn't leave work. A decorator from a nation-wide chain of motels was coming to the showroom that afternoon to place a substantial order of very durable and expensive wallpaper. His father needed him there. He suggested I ask his mother but I knew I couldn't call his mother. Belle had no sympathy for me: She felt sorrier for Phillip because *I* was sick than for me. I called Paul instead.

"You'll see," I said to Phillip, "it'll be a nice evening."

"Well, you're in charge," he said.

"Of what?"

"The evening."

The fire took hold; quivering shadows played on the window

drapes. Phil moved the Christmas tree into the corner of the room and cleared magazines and papers off the coffee table, and I went into the kitchen and tasted the warm cider and threw in more cinnamon.

Minutes later from the window I watched Paul and Vicki coming up the path in the light of the outdoor carriage lamp. Bundled in hats, mufflers, and boots, they were like two little Christmas carolers. Paul wasn't wearing his Persian lamb fur hat. The close-fitting woolen cap over which he'd wrapped a scarf babushka-style made him look as much like an old peasant woman as a middle-aged man, but it was clear that he'd loved the walk.

While he tried taking off his boots, I heard a raspish whistle in his breath. He kicked at the heel of his right boot impatiently. Phil helped him out of his overcoat. "Go easy on that coat," he warned. He pulled a round bowl out of his pocket and handed it to me and I sat down on the couch letting the bowl rest on my lap. Paul stretched out his hands to the fireplace—white hands, almost waxen. In a while I stood up, went over to Paul and put my arm around his back, clasping him affectionately. "Thanks for the bowl, Paul."

He yanked free of my arm and moaned, "Ohhh . . . not there," and his body tensed and his face contorted with pain. He reached his hand around his ribs and pressed his fingers against his back. It was so hard to look. My friend was fragile, my friend was dying. I couldn't believe that.

I winced as though I'd been slapped hard across the face, although the truth of course was that I'd hurt him. "I'm sorry." He didn't hear me. "I'm sorry," I repeated, this time more desperately. No response. I was stranded in front of the fireplace, a reprimanded child. By this time Paul was loosening up and scanning the room for a comfortable chair, but I'd been slapped into another country. The sting stayed with me while I brought Paul's and Vicki's coats into the bedroom and gave my hair a few hard strokes with the hairbrush. I had to believe that my friend was fragile, my friend was dying, and that I was losing him. Part of me never wanted to step foot in that living room again.

When I finally came out, Phil was serving the hot cider and telling the Miners about the tie-up at Penn Station and the almost-drunken camaraderie on the commuter train back to Huntstown. Some guy was offering the passengers bourbon in paper cups. "Did you take it?" Vicki asked. "I didn't, but Dad did," Phil said. "My father's been taking that train for over thirty years," Phillip said. "You'd be surprised how many guys walk through the car and say, 'How's it goin', Roger?'" Phil rambled on about his father—how in a way his father had "discovered" Huntstown, knowing immediately that some day his modest real estate investment would pay off big-time. Phil described the Huntstown of his childhood, when it was still country—even farmers, even cows. Phil was babbling on, keeping ahead of his fear. I don't think he'd ever known anyone who'd died. Both his parents were still living. "God, Huntstown must have been a beautiful place then," Paul said. He held his cup loosely, as though it were too heavy for him. It angled to the side and I thought the cider was going to dribble out and that Paul wouldn't even know it.

For a few minutes no one said anything. Time seemed a dangerous topic. Like a child, I was still nursing my wound. Let Phil take over. He was doing a fine job of it. I was waiting for some sign from Paul that I was reinstated in his affections but Paul didn't glance my way. He began to speak about his own past, a poor childhood in Hell's Kitchen, years of factory work and union organizing, night school, a slow start. "I'm just beginning to learn my trade," he said sadly, "and I'd like a few more years . . ." "Hey, it's not over till it's over," Phillip pronounced. "I'm sure you'll have a few more innings."

Phil's clichés seemed to cheer Paul, who turned to Phillip and asked him to put some music on the stereo.

Phil hid his surprise. "Brahms? Rock? Oldies?"

"Oldies tonight." Paul's voice was low. He rested his mug on the coffee table, leaning back against the high upholstered chair that cocooned him. I didn't want to think this but I did: that Paul looked like my poor old Grandma Doland after her stroke—the prominent nose in a thin face, the skin dull and gray, not reflecting light.

The fire burned, the flames drawn higher by an invisible draft. The room turned cozy. Frank Sinatra sang "Stormy Weather." I noticed Vicki, who had been sipping her drink, give Paul a quick, desperate look, then become slack and withdrawn.

"Most of the time I like rock," Paul said, "but not tonight." He sighed. "I must seem like an old man. Always *kvetching* about something." I remembered that Paul liked to use Yiddish words although he wasn't Jewish. His father, he had once told us, worked for years in a Jewish bakery. He knew how to make bagels. Paul was turning his head slowly from side to side, movements I couldn't decipher. A couple of moments later he hoisted himself out of the chair and came over to me. "Harriet, dance?"

"My pleasure." I tried to sound delighted, but I wished that he'd asked Vicki. In many ways he slighted his wife, was more generous to friends and strangers than to his own family.

Paul guided me to the center of the room and took me around

in the same gentle, loose way he'd held the mug. This time I held him lightly, as though my hand were a bird that couldn't quite land. "You look soft tonight," he whispered in my ear. "Dark green is your color." He was patting my back, gently, imperceptibly, with that translucent hand. Slowly we moved to the shadowy side of the room. I was sure that the snow had stopped. Paul's body was disappearing. Slowly, little by little, Paul was leaving us all. He was spinning away beyond reach. I tried not to give Paul the full weight of my arm; I felt his hand on my back, firm now. He pressed his cheek against mine. He whispered my name in my ear, that clunky, plain name — Harriet. We danced well together, or should I say we swayed well together. I made no sudden movements. I willed myself weightless. *"Stormy weather since my gal and I ain't together . . ."* I closed my eyes. I didn't think about Phillip and Vicki. I didn't know what they were doing; they weren't dancing. Phil didn't like dancing.

Gently, gently I folded in against Paul, what was left of my friend. There was scarcely any heat coming from his body, only a heartbeat. What a fool I'd been! Last Christmas at a family dinner at the Minerses', Paul and I found ourselves alone in the doorway between the kitchen and the dining room under a sprig of mistletoe. We could see that no one else was in either room. Paul pulled me against him and kissed me hard, his tongue sliding into my mouth. We clung to each other for a few moments. I became aroused — I know he did — and I remember feeling that that was wonderful because all those lines between love and friendship and lust and sweetness were blurred. This is how life should be, I thought, and wished we could find some empty room and lie down and touch each other, make love if we wanted to. But we couldn't, we didn't, and we never would. At the time we kissed and eventually pulled apart. I don't think anyone saw us. At any rate, we were safe. We were under the mistletoe.

"Stormy Weather" ended, "That Old Black Magic" began. Frank Sinatra. I opened my eyes and spotted Matina's little face peering around the corner of the doorway. She was watching Paul and me curiously. When Paul noticed her, he let go of me and took her hand and led her to the couch next to Vicki. "What are you doing up, Matina?" he asked; his voice was sweet, his response quicker than mine; I was still caught in some black-magic spell. Matina was the last person I wanted to see. But Paul and Vicki, who had no children, were always gentle with ours.

"I couldn't fall asleep," she told Paul. "Is it the new year yet?"

"Not yet, sweetheart. Here, sit between Vicki and me." Paul snuggled her between them and reached over to the coffee table and gave her a handful of nuts and raisins. Matina, in her woolly pink pajamas, adored being the only child in the room. Paul checked his watch and I glanced at mine; it was only nine-thirty and midnight was an eternity away. From Paul's expression I assumed he felt the same way, but then he brightened. "Tonight the new year comes early—at ten," he announced.

"Like a baby who can't wait to be born," Phillip added, squatting in front of the fire, his back to us. The logs crumbled into glowing chunks as he poked at them. He stood up and headed for the porch.

When Phil came back with an armload of wood, Matina jumped up from the couch to help him put a log on the fire. In her eagerness her arm and hand brushed over the coffee table and tipped the bowl of nuts and bumped Paul's new bowl, which rolled over the edge and crashed onto the bare wooden floor.

"Matina!" Phil yelled. His arm jerked up as though he were going to smack her, but of course he didn't. He'd never hit her. "Uncle Paul's bowl! Look at it!" he yelled. His voice was rough. "You've broken it, for chrissakes!" I had never seen him explode so violently.

Matina began to heave and sob.

I stood there, couldn't move.

"It's okay, Matina, it's okay," Paul soothed, but she couldn't stop crying. She pulled her pajama top over her face. Muffled, her sobs echoed louder. "It's okay, sweetheart. A bowl is just a ball of mud shaped a little and baked, that's all. It's not meant to last forever." He patted Matina on the back and turned to Phillip. "Phil, it's no big deal. You're being too harsh." Matina was gulping air now.

"Uncle Paul will make us another bowl," I managed to whisper.

"I have another one at home—a larger one. I'll bring it over the next time I come."

I kneeled down on the floor trying to gather up the pieces and fit them together, but there were too many pieces. I held the fragments in my hand not knowing what to do with them.

"Don't cry, sweetheart," Paul said again, and Matina put her hand on his knee. "Here, sit up on my lap," Paul said. "Sit right up here on my knees evenly, in the middle." Gently Matina balanced herself on his lap. "Don't lean back, sweetheart." He repeated that. "Don't lean back." He held her and kissed the top of her head. Matina sat precariously on the edge of his lap. She looked uncomfortable.

I carried the broken pieces into the kitchen. Phil followed me. "I shouldn't've yelled at her," he whispered. "That was a mistake. I lost it." "We're all a little on edge tonight," I said, my anger dissipating. "You're always patient," Phillip said with genuine awe. "An occupational liability," I explained. "I was trained to be patient." My fingertips tapped Phil's arm. "You were kind to Paul and Vicki." The two of us stood in the kitchen caught up in the far-too-obvious symbolism of the smashed bowl, and neither of us wanted to leave the kitchen. "No matter," Phillip said, "we should've insisted that Matina go to bed at her usual time." I agreed. Matina tested the limits of our patience, mine as well as Phil's.

In the living room the mood was calm, normal. Vicki and Paul and Matina were talking. Matina was explaining why the things that Paul made were not balls of mud. "They're made of clay," she insisted.

"Clay is mud, honey," Paul explained. "Clay is earth. I can take you to a beach at Lighthouse Point and show you a hillside of clay. We can dig some up and take it home and put it on the wheel and turn it and turn it and raise up its sides and make that ball of mud into a bowl. And then we can fire it in the kiln and it'll turn into something very hard and very lasting."

As Paul described the process, I could see him working at the wheel. I loved his concentration. I loved watching his hands draw up the soft wet walls of clay. I loved that process of turning a slippery, wet ball of mud into a bowl, and mostly I loved how Paul went into a trance, with his eyes partly closed; he was there but he wasn't there. And his lips moved into a tiny, almost invisible smile, as though he were truly pleased that at his advanced age he'd learned a whole new set of tricks, a craft.

"If it's so hard, why did it break?" Matina asked.

"Enough questions!" Phil said with exasperation, his face yielding to gloom. A shadowy thought danced across the screen of my mind: that Phillip was angry at me, not at Matina. *I* pressed against the limits of *his* patience. I shouldn't have danced with Paul.

"Hey, it's getting close to the new year," I announced, determined to move the evening along, determined to rescue whatever cheer was possible. "How about some champagne?" My watch showed 9:55. Vicki and Paul turned down the champagne. Paul looked worn out. It was ten o'clock, our designated time for the new year's arrival.

The words *Happy New Year* hung in the air unclaimed, like old party decorations.

I stood up and extended my hand to Paul and gently, so gently, drew him up from the couch. Then Paul reached out to Phillip who motioned to Vicki; and Matina, seeing that a circle was forming, joined it. We put our arms around each other, Vicki and I flanking Paul, holding him lightly, swaying ever so slightly from side to side. We were in a huddle, the five of us; no one spoke, not even Matina. I rested my hand on Paul's back gently, so gently, and I closed my eyes. The boundaries of time and space and real life blurred. I wanted them to.

Then I sailed right through the picture window and carried that light-boned body outside and lifted my friend up into the glowing violet night. We were flying, Paul and I, and I carried him over the tops of trees, their branches holding strong under the weight of snow. We swooped down over the gentle rounds of hills beyond the golf course. I held him lightly; the flight was a caress and a loving, and he was no heavier than a silk robe. We sailed over the ragged edges of land, over estuaries and salt marshes with last summer's cattails. We flew over highways veiled by snow, and white rooftops and uncluttered stretches of field, smooth and sparkling and porcelain white. I kissed Paul's mouth and my kiss was a snowflake on his lips. I flew with him in my arms and the flight was nothing more, nothing less than an embrace, and then I brought him back and set him down.

Finally Phillip broke the circle and headed toward the kitchen. I opened my eyes and turned to Paul. He was neither happy nor cured. He checked his watch, this time making no disguise of that gesture. He and Vicki declined the tea and cake I offered them.

It was hard to watch Vicki kneeling at Paul's feet struggling to get his boots on him. Then Phillip knelt down and signaled Vicki to move aside. I was glad that Phil was helping Paul, who sat there holding his breath, waiting for Phillip to finish. Matina stood in front of Paul, her face tilted toward his, waiting for a kiss. Everyone was waiting for something. Paul didn't notice. Finally Vicki said, "Paul, Matina wants to kiss you good night." He kissed the child perfunctorily and Matina backed away and turned to me. I picked her up and held her tightly. Paul leaned toward me but avoided touching me or letting me touch him. "Take good care of Phillip," he whispered in my ear.

Take good care of Phillip! I sucked in my breath. My face burned. Why did Phillip need to be taken care of?

Paul held on to Vicki as they made their way down the path. For a moment or two I watched them from the porch window. Then I grabbed my jacket and ran after them, tapping Paul on the arm, drawing him aside. "Take good care of Phillip! What did you mean by that? Don't we all need care? Doesn't each one of us need protection?" Paul stared at me. Vicki was gently tugging him toward the car. He stopped moving, stood absolutely still. If he'd had reasons for saying what he did, he couldn't find the words now. When he finally spoke his voice was barely audible. "I don't know why I said that, Harriet. I'm sorry." His apology caught me off guard. I didn't expect an apology.

We stood facing each other. It had stopped snowing, the night was crystal clear. He touched me lightly on the cheek with his gloved hand, his eyes resting on my face. "Dear girl," he whispered, then paused; "and you look like a beautiful, dear young girl tonight." His gaze was startlingly tender. He drew a breath, a difficult breath outside in the cold night. "'Try to love each other'—that's what I should have said."

I wanted to put my arm around him but this time I didn't dare.

Phillip drove the Miners home, and I put Matina to bed. Tired now, she was ready to sleep. I tiptoed into Eric's room and covered him, murmuring, "Happy New Year, my baby, my darling."

I closed Eric's door and went downstairs and poked at the sputtering fire. I was about to clear the mugs off the coffee table when I glanced down. Matina had dropped a small stuffed animal, a soft pink piggy, which I picked up. There were stray cashew nuts, too, a few raisins, and a piece of Paul's bowl under the couch. It was an odd-shaped fragment, almost a trapezoid, its edges sharp. I held that shard in my hand, then I put it in the pocket of my skirt—that piece of hardened mud, that bit of earth, that gift.

What I Learned from Clara

Clara was sitting on an aluminum lawn chair in the scrubby rectangle of our shared backyard, combing and brushing Sissy's blond hair. Sissy—her yappy, pampered Pomeranian. From the second-floor landing, I could see that Clara had brought out an extra lawn chair, and that chair waited for me hungrily. I tiptoed back into our apartment, shut the door, and put off taking Eric downstairs until later when Clara was gone. I did not want to see her. I did not want to talk to her. I did not want to hear her stories, even though I had the feeling that someday her stories might save my life.

It was early September and we were frying in the heat in Richmond, Virginia, where we had recently moved from the north. We lived in a five-room second-floor apartment in a plain, almost shabby neighborhood. We liked the apartment and we liked Mr. Gates, our landlord, and the rent turned out to be less than we had expected.

The kitchen window was shaded by the drooping branches of an enormous willow oak that softened and filtered the view across the street of a gloomy row of four-story apartment houses. Our kitchen table edged close up against the window. Matina, who was seven, often said, "Why do all of us look out the window so much? At home we didn't." Home had been Huntstown, a suburb on Long Island, a house that we didn't sell but rented to a retired couple.

It was true, Matina's observation. Neither Phillip nor I nor Eric in his high chair seemed able to take our eyes off the street below. Things were happening out there that never happened on Grantwood Lane in Huntstown. Police cars screamed to a stop and cops rushed into the apartment house across the street. A fire truck had already visited that building twice. Once a large U-Haul truck double parked all day while three young women in halter tops unloaded furniture and cartons. Occasionally I spotted Clara walking splayfooted and slowly down the street, a white plastic pocketbook and a bag of groceries in her hands.

Meanwhile, Eric's face was a smeary red from tomato sauce, and so were his hands and his plump little forearms. He was standing up in his high chair leaning over the back of it, about to tumble over. Phil kept a hand on him while I washed him off with a wad of paper towels. Then we set him free and he toddled into the living room.

I took out a pitcher of iced tea and instantly Matina wanted to know whether there were really tea trees. We were always explaining things to Matina and our answers never seemed to satisfy her.

"Yes, in India and Asia," Phillip answered, improvising, I assumed, but sounding authoritative. He took Matina's questions seriously, hated squeaking by with skimpy answers. "We need to find out more about India," he said.

•   •   •

We moved to Richmond because Phillip wanted to try living in a place that was new to him, away from his parents and Huntstown where he'd been born. There'd been times when he'd complained of feeling stodgy and dull, trapped in his father's life. And he was tired of working for his dad, who owned a small but high-quality wallpaper company that his grandfather had started in 1911. When Ralph Townsend, an old friend of Phil's from Pratt, begged Phil to join the advertising department of Eastland Pharmaceutical in Richmond, Phil said, "This is my chance to strike out on my own."

I was also ready for a change. I had been wearing thin from the normal household chores plus hairsplitting time schedules, being with the kids and arranging and driving to child care and job, which happened also to involve children, insofar as I'd become the director of three programs for nursery-age children with special needs in Suffolk county. Our days had become too rushed, too frantic.

A couple of years of not working: We'd live on a tight budget so I could enjoy my own children. I'd spend more time with Eric, who was so easygoing and sweet. Perhaps I'd rethink what kind of work I really wanted to do for the rest of my life. Recently, in trying to explain the Civil War to Matina, and why the South found their way of life worth dying for, I imagined going to graduate school and studying American history. I believed in new beginnings, years ahead of me, everything a matter of choosing. I was young. I couldn't bear the idea of not choosing.

Besides, everyone around us in New York was divorcing or dying, at least that's how it had seemed to us at the time. We were so young, everything and everyone seemed to be falling apart. As soon as we made good friends, they either moved away or split up.

Then Paul Miner, one of our best friends, died of lung cancer. He was forty-seven; we weren't even thirty then. Paul had been a ceramist on the verge of modest success, a man whom we admired, and who I think loved us. Yes, *loved*. By that I mean he seemed to know what each of us was capable of—the best in us.

The day we moved into our apartment in Richmond the temperature was ninety-eight degrees, a heat that was hardly unusual, clearly a fact of life, I was told. I remember I'd worn a loose dress around the apartment while we unpacked. Drops of sweat were rolling off my body and from under my breasts and stinging the tops of my bare feet. At first I didn't realize it was sweat. I kept looking up at the ceiling, sure that there were leaking pipes, but there were no leaking pipes.

Mr. Gates, our landlord, told us that the two small apartments on the first floor had been rented over the summer to Billy Redmond from West Virginia and to Mrs. Ames, an elderly woman from Norfolk, and her Pomeranian. On our first day the door of Billy's apartment stood open for the "cross-breeze," he explained as he introduced himself. One hand was holding an iron. He was a young man with a pleasant pink face. The only furniture I noticed in his apartment was an ironing board. Billy was about to iron a white shirt and a black lightweight suit. A black tie hung on the doorknob.

We met Mrs. Ames on our second morning in Richmond. She was about eighty years old, more or less. She asked us to call her Clara, and introduced us to Sissy. "I hope the children won't bother Sissy," she said, and then as an afterthought added, "I hope Sissy doesn't snap at them." I thought, here is a woman who loves her dog more than she likes people, and at first I didn't like *her*. Magnified through the thick lenses of her glasses, her eyes seemed large and colorless and seemed to have lost interest in seeing. It was as though I were peering right through her head and out to the hazy, humid day.

For the first month or two in Richmond, I walked Matina to school—it was named after Robert E. Lee—with Eric in his stroller, and then I did my marketing in the neighborhood. Sometimes I took Eric to a nearby park where he could play in a sandbox. Often when Eric and I returned to our house around noon, Clara had her door open and she'd urge me to stop in for a few minutes. One day she showed me how she cooked a loin of pork and potatoes and green beans in gravy, and how she made up small aluminum pie plates filled with the food and covered them with tinfoil and froze them, her own homemade TV dinners. "What a good idea!" I said, or "It certainly smells delicious around here." Clara tried to get us to stay for a little visit, but I told her that the good smells were making Eric hungry for his lunch.

In the afternoons I'd explore the neighborhood with Eric in his stroller. I liked discovering Civil War monuments in unexpected places, small fenced-in islands where streets intersected, with statues of Jeb Stuart on horseback or Stonewall Jackson. I liked seeing new kinds of trees, the willow oaks and the glossy-leafed magnolias in the afternoon sun. Often I would stop the stroller and pull Eric into my arms and hold him up against the sky and then kiss him, and put my cheek against his. Eric and I would be waiting for Matina in the school yard at three o' clock, and when I saw her my heart would soar. Her long, thick dark hair, her sturdy little body, her mind still chewing over some piece of information culled from a lesson given by her teacher, Mrs. Chase. On the walk home Matina would pat Eric's head and kiss his cheek while we waited for the light to change at the corner. My eyes would tear from joy, my heart filled with love. I was happy not to hear about the latest wrinkle in some friend's deteriorating marriage or how someone had had a breakthrough in their consciousness-raising group.

My life seemed uncomplicated, although Matina was always sufficiently complicated to keep me from thinking I was on a holiday. Dealing with Matina was time-consuming; it took patience. It took a kind of discipline and steadiness which I was realizing, little by little, was what being a mother meant. The daily routine—no weekends off, no sabbaticals. However, in spite of Matina's nature, which was not "bad" but simply demanding, my life was less stressful than it had been in the North. I had no job, no rigorous schedule, no house or lawns to maintain, no social life to sustain. I was floating. I wasn't moving forward. Sometimes I felt as if I was sliding backward, as though I'd left the women's movement and politics and the seventies in the North, and I was living the life my mother lived before my father left us. I was a housewife, and I did my marketing—even the word *marketing* smacks of earlier times—at a neighborhood store and at the bakery the way my mother had when I was very small. Stan, the silver-haired butcher, explained about Smithfield ham, how the pigs were raised on peanuts. "How's *the Northerner* on this fine day?" he would ask when he saw me, and then give Eric a lollipop.

For the first time in my life I wasn't eager to make new friends. It was as though I were "filled" with all the people I'd ever known. Family members and dear friends, even ones who'd died, were alive to me, and I could close my eyes and see them: my suntanned father in the crisp, white, short-sleeved shirt he wore at the beach when we strolled in the evenings; my mother's sweet, thin hands as she held potatoes and peeled them in a flash; Paul in his black fur hat on the frozen pond in Huntstown. Those people from my past and the new neighborhood were enough for now. The various shades of brick or the architecture of the nearby homes or the beauty of a small church intrigued me more than Ralph Townsend, Phil's friend at Eastland, or Nick and Eva Stratton, whom Ralph and his wife, Maxine, had introduced us to. At that time there was nothing I wanted from them, and I felt in danger of their demands. That sounds terrible, but it was the truth: for a short while I wanted nothing demanded of me.

In that way I was trying to be different from my mother and the life she'd led before my father left us. My mother never cut herself off from what she imagined other people needed, and her imagination was very alive in that department. Even after my father left, my mother tended to his mother, Grandma Doland, trying to soothe her loss, trying to make up to my grandmother for her son's bad behavior, trying to cheer her up. Or maybe my mother was simply grasping onto whatever was left of my father, holding tight to her old life. My mother knew only one story: a vague sort of romance. She stuck to it like glue.

Once when we made dinner for Ralph and Maxine and the Strattons, I was startled when Nick, an attractive man with sexy gray eyes, asked me if he could borrow a book that he saw on our bookshelf. It was a novel from a college English course I had once taken. What startled me was my reluctance to lend it to him and my sense that his request was an unfair demand. To be honest—and I'm not proud of this—that's how I saw Clara's claim on my time and attention.

One day Clara heard us open the downstairs front door as we entered the hallway. "I just got this picture of my son in the mail," she said, holding out a picture of a well-dressed, balding man whom I considered elderly, someone in his fifties or maybe his sixties. "Lives in Omaha," she said. "Works for an insurance company. I had six children in my time, four still living. Three husbands." Not wanting to encourage more confidences, I didn't say anything. Maybe I murmured, "Three husbands . . ." in a whisper that Clara could barely hear. Sissy began to yap and circle the children, and Clara bent over slowly and picked her up; and the bending over and picking up was an effort. "Harriet, I want to tell you something. I'll be working two afternoons and two nights a week," she told me, "so don't be worried about me if you don't see my lights on Tuesday and Friday nights. I'm taking care of an old woman over on River Street. Saw the job listed in the newspaper."

"She's a very fine woman," Clara said of her *charge*, Miss Claudia Taylor. "She's frail and needs someone to be there with her. She's eighty-four. She can't do for herself. She's weak but clear-minded. Clear-minded or not, I don't want to live that long. Life is good only when you're holding the reins."

I tried to picture Miss Claudia Taylor and it was difficult to imagine someone older than Clara.

"I've got to give these kids a snack and think about dinner," I said to her while Matina bounded up the stairs to our apartment and Sissy barked. Clara turned and moved awkwardly back into her own small apartment. I followed Matina, and Eric followed me, up two steps and down one, as though stairs were a great game. And when I waited for Eric somewhere midway on the stairs I could see into Billy Redmond's apartment. I could see him ironing a pair of black trousers. He was an apprentice to morticians.

During our first year, Phillip and I had enjoyed setting up a new home, making the children comfortable, making the apartment attractive. Phillip felt some immediate victory in leaving his father's business and his parents' bailiwick. His new job involved traveling occasionally to the company's main office outside of Atlanta, and also to a branch in Maryland, and initially he enjoyed the freedom of moving about, of leaving the children and me. I even liked his brief absences. He was cheerful when he returned home. That made up for the time he was gone. He was easygoing, buoyant, pleased with himself in a good way. His clothes became brighter and more playful—wide ties with flowers in violet and green and shades of pink; a bright red button-down shirt. He grew a mustache.

Being cut loose from the old life and its familiarity and its proximity to family and long-standing obligations had a loosening effect on our sex life. We could make love on top of the sheets because the weather was so hot, or on the carpet in the living room, listening to music. Surprisingly, the heat made us frisky, and sex seemed like a truly fine entertainment, one of the most interesting entertainments in Richmond. After one trip Phillip said, "If this is what it's like to come home, I'll have to go away at least every week."

By our second year in Richmond nothing that much had changed. I'd made no friends. I'd heard of no organization or group that I wanted to join, no job I wanted to inquire about. Of course I didn't look for those opportunities, and they don't tend to parade up to you and present themselves. We left our New York plates on our car and kept our New York drivers' licenses. We didn't take delivery of the city newspaper.

Billy Redmond and Clara remained our neighbors. The ironing board in Billy's apartment was no longer visible when his door was open. He still wore black suits and white shirts and black ties, but now I saw him carrying plastic bags from the dry cleaner's, a sign of his growing success. Clara continued her weekly bouts of cooking—I could smell the bacon and pork—making her own TV dinners and taking them with her once in a while, she told me in the downstairs hall, to share with Miss Taylor. "I love working," Clara said. "I've always worked, always earned my money. I was a spinner once for five years at a textile mill near Concord, North Carolina. Did I ever tell you about that?"

On one particularly fine autumn afternoon Clara spotted Eric and me in the backyard. Eric was scooting along on a small blue-and-red painted horse that had a red cart attached to it. Clara waved and soon appeared with one of her lawn chairs. I noticed that she had also managed to carry out a large photograph album. "Go into my apartment, dear, and behind the door is the other lawn chair. Bring it out so that you can sit down. I want to show you some pictures. I'll keep my eye on Eric. He's a good boy."

I'll keep my eye on Eric. I did what Clara asked me to do. I found the lawn chair. But her words made me think of Paul, my friend who'd died—Paul, our neighbor in Huntstown. I recalled how once when I was sick with strep throat and Phil was at work, Paul, who was healthy at that time, had come over to our house and offered to keep an eye on Eric for the afternoon. Paul had given me an entire afternoon to sleep. It was something a mother would have done, or a sister, or a woman friend. At that time my mother had recently died, I had no sister, and all my women friends were either working or lived in distant places. Phillip couldn't take a day off from work because his dad needed him at the showroom. I was especially grateful for a man who would offer to help me. Thinking about Paul had shaken me—not in a bad way, but in a way I liked. I felt gratitude and self-pity. That I had had such a friend, that I had lost him. Right before Clara called out my name again, I was wishing that I had slept with Paul. Not because of desire. But because of uncovering and revealing. Because of friendship.

What were Clara's photographs all about?

I tried to concentrate on the pictures. Sissy, leashed to the arm of Clara's chair, was yapping. Eric was happily unloading his cart of worldly possessions. Family photographs are interesting only if they're your own family, or the family of someone you love. The thought of wading through the life histories of Clara's six children pressed on me. It could take hours.

Lo and behold the pictures were mostly of Clara herself. Of when she was a young woman: shots of her on a horse, or poised with a bow and arrow, or in a cap and gown graduating, at the seaside in a black bathing suit with a long skirt. There was a wedding picture that she tried to flip by quickly. "You were beautiful," I said, and I stopped her from turning the page. She had indeed been a stately bride. "Brides all look alike to me," Clara said. "They look so hopeful and sweet . . . and a little silly." She chuckled. Then she turned a few pages and came to a photograph of herself with a line of young children and a group of men, a bunch on each side of her in front of a big old house with balconies and porches. "This was the boardinghouse I ran in Scranton, P. A., after I left my second husband. That's how *I* raised my children, Harriet. Always did everything myself. Liked it, actually."

"Why did you leave your second husband?"

"Don't know. Honestly I'm not sure. Maybe because he was grouchy, and I thought, 'We only have one life to lead and why muddy it up with someone else's bad moods. He seemed all too happy to live his life under a black cloud, and I wasn't. I suppose that's why," and Clara reached down and picked up Sissy and put her on her lap and petted her. The dog stopped yapping. "I don't know . . ." Clara said. "I guess that's why." And Clara lighted up one of her Marlboros and smoked, and stared into the distance, across the yard, across the street, across the small city, across the vast battlefields of the Confederacy, not seeing a blessed thing. And she was quiet for a moment or two, and I thought we'd come to the end of that subject, but she started up again. "I never did divorce my third husband," she said. "He's still my husband. I like the man. I go see him once in a while. In Roanoke. I make him my famous fried chicken. Help him out when he's sick."

I was getting restless. Matina would be home from school soon. I wanted to go, but Clara detained me. She wanted to tell me about the boardinghouse, how many thousands of meals she had cooked and how the men loved her *homecookin'*—mostly miners. She wanted to tell me how hard she had worked, how she had thrived on it. I believed at the time that she wanted to show me her whole damn life, hold it out for me in the palm of her hand, and have me examine it, admire it, hear every detail about it. The strange part was that I did admire her. But still, I didn't want to hear every detail. I noticed that her dress was soiled with food stains, grease spots. I noticed that she had a bandage on her leg. I noticed how round her eyes looked, and how yellow in the afternoon light. I'm only thirty-two years old, I said to myself, and it felt like Clara was hammering herself into my head. I had two children to raise, and one was still a toddler. I didn't want to hear how strong she'd been in the face of adversity, or how totally on her own she'd managed everything. The message of all her stories, I believed at the time, was that she was strong and I was weak, that she had "character" and I didn't, and that the reason she did was because she'd been tested and I hadn't. I wanted to say, *I've been tested, too*, but I didn't dare because it was too early in the game: I didn't know what other tests the future held for me and whether I'd pass them.

"Eric and I have to go and pick up Matina at school," I said, standing up. "I enjoyed seeing your pictures, Clara." "I have another album I want to show you," she told me.

As winter came Phillip had to go on more business trips to Maryland and Atlanta, and a couple of trips to New York City to work on promotion for a pharmaceutical convention. While he was in New York he saw his folks, and his father begged him to come back into the business, offering him more money, more autonomy. The business was expanding in interesting ways: Japan was manufacturing extraordinarily high-quality wallpaper; Phillip could head up a new import operation. His father *needed* him; Eastland Pharmaceutical didn't. Phil was tempted.

Actually, living in Richmond was not growing more appealing to either of us. Phillip's trips were increasingly disruptive, and Eric and Matina got upset when they saw him packing his suitcase. Also, the Robert E. Lee school wasn't wearing well.

One evening, when Phil was in Maryland, Nick Stratton called. He finally wanted to return the book he had borrowed from me almost a year ago. Nine-thirty? It seemed oddly late. The children were already asleep.

I showered and put on a violet-colored skirt and a white sweater. I'd shed the last of the poundage I had gained from both pregnancies.

Nick arrived with my book and an assortment of small packages, a bottle of wine, a record. "I remember that you said you liked

Johnny Mathis, The Platters, Nat King Cole, so I brought over some albums. Keep them as long as you want," he said. "I certainly was delinquent with that novel."

"You have a good memory," I said, and then asked him what he thought of the book.

"I couldn't get into it. Too slow-moving, I guess; too low-key."

His voice had a pleasing, almost professorial resonance. He had nothing important to say.

"I remember loving it," I said.

"I'm embarrassed to have had the book for so long and not to have read it," Nick admitted.

I didn't smile. I said nothing reassuring. I remembered wondering why he'd borrowed the book in the first place. I remembered how I didn't want to lend it to him—perhaps because I knew he didn't really want to read it, and that he'd offer nothing in return. It had been a time for me of keeping accounts, unattractive as that might seem; there are those times, however, when you feel you don't have enough to give away. Times when you don't have an endless supply of goodwill, when you're going through something you can't even name. I think people should be forgiven for those times.

"How come you borrowed the book in the first place?" I finally asked.

Grinning, he unfolded comfortably in his chair, stretching out his legs, his gray eyes on me. I waited for his answer. There was a moment or two of silence. "I didn't know why then, but now I do: so I could return it."

I smiled, I couldn't help it. The wine he had brought was an expensive one, and he suggested that we open the bottle. I felt awkward. He found the wineglasses in the kitchen cupboard. He had brought along a corkscrew. We drank wine at the kitchen table. There was a wedge of good cheese in one of the packages, some tangerines in the other.

Nick put the record he had brought on the stereo and asked me if I wanted to dance. I said no, then changed my mind. The children were sound asleep. Dancing had been ecstasy for me when I was younger. Phillip didn't understand dancing. The body as vehicle, not for the mind or the person but for movement itself, as though the body were a deer or an airplane or a shooting star.

Nick and I danced. To both sides of the record. We danced to an old Frank Sinatra album. We danced close, and we "dipped." We laughed at ourselves. Nick loved to dance, a fact that surprised me because Phillip had convinced me long ago that guys didn't care for dancing, that dancing was like Valentine's Day or lacy wedding gowns, girlish and sweet and silly. I never thought I'd dance again, this kind of slow dancing. I liked resting my hands on his shoulders. I liked how his hand felt on the small of my back. Nick was an attractive man, with his remarkable gray eyes. He never offered to be my friend, and I could see that he wouldn't make a good friend. Besides, I didn't want him as a friend. I had many fine friends up North.

The music was as thick as fur, keeping out the street sounds. We danced well together, and when we got tired I sat on Nick's lap, and we kissed and necked, and took off our clothes and made love as though we were still dancing. And in a real sense we were. It had nothing at all to do with uncovering and revealing.

Three other times when Phillip was away on business trips Nick came over with a bottle of wine and a couple of records. Once he brought a bag of potato chips; another time two meatball subs. One night we made milkshakes. We snacked and we danced. Eric

woke up once; he cried but stayed in his bed. I went in and comforted him and stayed with him until he fell back to sleep. It
dawned on me after a while that Nick must have known, or sensed,
that Phil was not going to stay at Eastland for long, that Phil and I
were heading back North. Or perhaps he knew more than that,
that Phil was involved with someone at work, some secretary or
other employee. One of the secretaries, Janine, kept sending me
little trinkets—a key ring, a small sewing kit, a tiny lacquered box.
Why is this woman sending me these trinkets? I asked myself; and
my answer, unreasoned as it was, was that she was sleeping with
Phil. But perhaps not. It was as though what happened in Richmond didn't count; it wasn't our real life. I was on vacation from
the real me. It was "time-out," or some earlier time—back in history, like being a flapper in the twenties, or dancing the Lindy after
World War II, or wearing penny loafers in the fifties; some other
time, some faraway place where we didn't actually belong but were
floating through.

My shadow of suspicion about Phil had nothing to do with any
change in Phil's relationship to me, or how I experienced his feelings for me. I don't think he thought about me that much. He was
thinking about his father's offer to come back to the business,
about heading up the import division. The only note of criticism I
felt from Phil occurred after he met Clara in the downstairs hallway and she showed him the sore on her leg and how it wasn't
healing. She'd been soaking it, putting ointment on it, dressing it.
He told Clara that I would take her to see a doctor, and when he
told me what he'd said, I frowned—an expression of dismay.
"Really, Harriet . . ." Phil said, with exasperation.

"Why don't we both go with her," I suggested. It was Phil's turn
to frown.

"I've already been to a doctor," Clara said when I finally offered to take her the next day. "Two weeks ago. It didn't do any good." She pulled back the bandage and showed me the oozing, infected sore. It was triangular, and reminded me of an animal bite. "Did Sissy bite you?" I asked. "No," Clara said, "I bumped into the corner of the coffee table." "It looks bad, Clara. I'm going to take you to see our doctor. You need antibiotics." "People take too many of those drugs nowadays; weakens the system," Clara said, "and besides, I don't always do what people want me to do."

When I saw Clara the following week she was favoring the leg with the sore. "You have to see a doctor," I insisted, and once again she replied that she already had.

That night Phil was away in Baltimore and Nick came over at ten-thirty. The children were fast asleep and would stay that way, I hoped. It was the last time Nick came over, and I think at the time we both knew it would be. We were dancing, and because I enjoyed moving so easily, I found myself thinking about Clara — her slow, clumsy, splayfooted gait and now the additional limp and the obvious pain that moving involved. I imagined Clara's leg having to be amputated. I was sure of it, and I worried about her. Why didn't her children come and look after her? I thought about asking her that question, in a tactful way, of course.

And the next day I did. When Matina was in school, I took Eric downstairs with an armload of toys, and knocked on Clara's door. "The door's open," she called. She was watching a TV game show and smoking a cigarette. The bad leg was resting on the coffee table. The sore looked no worse; in fact, the bandage was smaller and neater, and the whole area looked less angry and infected. She confided that she had never returned to the doctor for a second visit. She knew how to treat an infection better than the doctor.

After all, she had nursed six children with their share of sores and wounds. Clara had led me right into my "topic."

"Clara, do you ever miss your children?"

She watched the game show as if she hadn't heard me, and took a drag on her cigarette. The bulky couch and armchair took up most of the space in the small living room. I asked Clara if I could bum a cigarette. "Of course, honey. Help yourself." She handed me her lighter which was in her dress pocket. "Would you like a pack to take upstairs?" I said no.

For a while Clara was quiet, then she began to talk. "My children are grown people now. I don't like to impose. Never have." She stopped.

"They come when they can. John came to Norfolk a couple of years ago. In fact he's the one gave me Sissy. Now where would I be without Sissy?" Clara appeared to be waiting for an answer, but I, of course, didn't have one, and she continued. "Lorraine writes me. Jimmy calls once in a while. He always sends me a plant on Mother's Day. He never forgets, but if he did I wouldn't hold it against him."

"Wouldn't it cheer you up if they visited?" I asked.

"What?"

"Seeing your children? Having them visit you more?"

She didn't answer right away. I enjoyed my cigarette. Eric was staring at the game show on TV.

"I don't hold it against them. They have their own lives to lead. You know I wasn't always such a fine mother. I had to work hard, didn't always pay attention. I sent their fathers packing. I liked cooking for all those sweet men. And then your children get older and become more like regular people. You go on loving them but there are times you don't always like them. Your children can't save you from your own life, Harriet. And only when you're young do you think you can save them. You've got to let people be who they are.

"In the end I think they've forgiven me, my children. They're not young anymore. Lorraine is going on sixty. And John gave me Sissy. Two of my children died—Roger and Cecily. Cecily was the smart one." She paused, then sighed. "You know, Harriet, you can't spend your whole life never saying good-bye. You got to say good-bye and get on with it."

"Where *is* Sissy, by the way?" I noticed the absence of yapping.

"I left her over at Miss Taylor's. Miss Taylor gets a big kick out of her. I'm going over there later myself."

Restless and hungry, Eric started pummeling me. I nestled my cheek against his; he pushed away. I stood up. At that moment I knew I wasn't like Clara: I adored my children, I always would. I'd always like them, too.

Clara stood up also, slowly, with effort. "No, I don't want my children coming here and trying to take care of me and having a whole bunch of opinions, and feeling sorry for me. I like doing for myself. Wait," she insisted, "and let me show you that other album."

I felt a sharp stabbing panic. "No, I can't stay. Thanks for the cigarette," I mumbled from the hallway.

I saw Clara once or twice in the next few days and then not at all for a while. Phillip and I were trying to figure out where we were going, what we were going to do.

We knew we were not going to stay in Virginia. "My father wants me to come back to the company," Phillip said at least twice a day. "What do you think, Harriet?" I said, "*You* have to decide what you want to do." A part of me waited for the other possibilities that

Phillip would come up with, but I didn't hear them. The good salary, the expanded autonomy, the security, the familiarity and continuity that his father's business offered blanked out any other ideas Phillip might have had. "It's time to put my feet on the ground," he said. I loved him with his feet slightly off the ground, or at least not on the ground all the time.

We were talking in the living room in the evening after Eric and Matina were asleep. A spring breeze had sucked one of the curtains out the window where it was waving like a flag. An ambulance pulled up to the row of houses across the street. We watched as two men carried a stretcher into the building. Phillip said, "You know I haven't seen any sign of life in Clara's apartment all week. I wonder if she's in the hospital."

It was hard for me to imagine Clara sick. "Maybe she's staying with the old lady she works for, Miss Taylor."

"I'm going downstairs and knock on her door," Phillip said.

"She works on Tuesdays and Fridays," I said, watching the scene across the street, waiting for the ambulance men to come out of the building with the stretcher.

"But today is Wednesday," Phillip reminded me.

For a few seconds we stood at the window and watched the ambulance attendants leave the building with the stretcher still empty. Each of us was relieved, I think. The building across the street was full of false alarms. Phillip went downstairs and knocked on Clara's door and returned. She wasn't there. I repeated my hunch that she was staying at Miss Taylor's, but Phillip remained doubtful and considered calling the two hospitals in our neighborhood. However, in the end he didn't.

We went to bed. I dreamed—not about Clara; I dreamed about my dear friend Paul. That we were ice-skating on a smooth, lustrous pond in Huntstown. It was a freezing day. I loved the cold. We were skating in long graceful glides, our arms crisscrossed in front of us. We were like great birds swooping and sailing on an airstream. Then I dreamed that I almost tripped on a narrow ridge in the ice, and I lurched in my sleep. I stopped skating. Made Paul stop. I leaned my whole body against his, I let my head rest against his shoulder. I woke up from that dream and couldn't fall back to sleep. It was only two A.M. I sat in the dark living room and missed Nick and said good-bye to him in my mind. I longed for my father, who left my mother and me when I was eight, and for Paul, to whom I should have been more loving and more revealing. I should have caressed Paul's body before that body became the source of so much pain, before that body disappeared.

I didn't think about Clara until the next evening. "I can't believe how unconcerned you are about her," Phillip said. "You knew the woman, you spent time with her, she was very fond of you."

"I did enough for her," I said. "I liked her but I didn't want to become responsible for her. I admired her self-sufficiency."

"No one's questioning that."

"I think *you* are," I said.

"I'm not questioning whether you did enough for her."

"What are *you* questioning then?"

"That something happened to her—and we don't even know."

"Well then, find out," I said. We had somehow moved into a time of not appreciating each other.

On Saturday morning Phillip called our landlord, Mr. Gates, to tell him that we wouldn't be renting the apartment past June. Phil was about to hang up. "Ask him about Clara," I whispered from across the room.

For a while Phillip was quiet, listening to Mr. Gates and not saying anything. His face became very still, his lips a straight line as he sucked them in. After he hung up he turned to me and said, "Clara was killed in a fire that broke out during the night at Miss Taylor's house. A week and a half ago. Both of them burned to death."

I remained still. I saw the flames consuming the two old women. I saw their dry white ashes.

"Gates was surprised we didn't know. It was in the newspaper." Phillip took a seat at the kitchen table. Matina came in and wanted to know what was wrong. We told her to go and play in her room and we would talk with her later.

For a few moments I thought about Clara. I saw her standing in her kitchen covering meat and vegetables with tinfoil. I saw her walking down the street, splayfooted, carrying her bag of groceries, hanging on to Sissy's leash. Sissy—yappy, pampered, beloved Sissy, a gift from her son John, the insurance man from Omaha.

Clara takes care of herself, I whispered under my breath. Clara gives what she can, and Clara moves on. For a moment or two I believed that Clara had set the fire.

Phillip turned to me and said that I didn't seem that shocked or upset. His tone was accusatory, as though I were somehow responsible for Clara's death. I stopped trying to defend myself: I wasn't responsible for Clara's death. But as I stood in the line of Phillip's cool gaze, my imagination performed a trick. Clara turned into a great black horse, difficult to handle and headstrong; and at the same time she was the rider. She was the horse *and* the rider.

I was learning to say good-bye . . . but to whom?

His Mother, His Daughter

Phillip's mother hadn't actually asked him to come out to Huntstown to hear her sing in the senior citizens' choral group. Phillip was the one who thought it would be a good idea to take his children, Matina and Eric, and go. "We're only amateurs," his mother told him on the phone, "and I'm afraid the children will be bored. Besides, you'll think we're foolish." Phillip objected. "Ma, we think what you're doing is amazing." And indeed he was amazed. It was the first time he had ever known his mother to do something outside the house, although she always used to tell him how much she loved working before he was born, forty-two years ago.

Phillip expected Matina, who was seventeen, to dress normally for her grandmother's debut, but *no*: an enormous silvery earring in the shape of an eight dangled from one ear, zebra-striped pants, a white T-shirt that looked dirty, rubbery pink plastic shoes and white socks with lacy cuffs on her feet. "What about a pair of regular jeans?" Her regular jeans, she explained, were at home. "At home" was Matina's small, to-be-counted-on jab to let him know that Harriet's—her mother's—apartment, and not his, was home. His apartment, still rather barren, she referred to as "your place."

At his place Matina never unpacked the medium-sized lavender-and-red nylon backpack in which she transported her clothes and schoolbooks. She took it into the bathroom when she changed clothes. There were things in it he wasn't allowed to see—hidden objects that comprised some kind of life-support system which neither he nor his apartment could provide. According to her brother, she was glued to that backpack with some kind of super epoxy.

"We have exactly sixteen minutes to catch the train," Eric announced.

He was the child who saw to it that time moved forward, and that they all moved forward with it. Ever since Harriet and he had separated, Eric grew tense when they had to be anywhere at a certain time. Often Matina made a scene when it was time to go, like having on the wrong clothes or deciding at the last minute that she didn't want to go at all. Everything got jumbled up. If they were late, Phillip had reassured the boy, it certainly wasn't his fault. And Harriet had gotten him a Walkman, hoping that his favorite music would calm him at those transitional moments. Sometimes it did.

Pennsylvania Station, which was only a short distance away, was walkable if Matina could be counted on to walk fast, but Phillip couldn't count on Matina's willingness to let him set the pace for anything. Matina didn't want things to proceed happily and easily without Harriet. Out of respect for her mother there had to be a period of limping and woundedness and awkwardness. He was beginning to understand that. They took a taxi. "We'll make it in good time," Eric said in the cab, his eyes never lifting from his digital watch. They made it with five minutes to spare.

On the train Matina looked squarely at her father. She had velvety gray eyes, and had recently mowed off her long, dark, rather wild hair and bleached what was left of it a pale blond. "Are you going to fix up your place, Dad, or are you coming back home?" He flinched. In her eyes he was still a misguided Odysseus who'd left home, and home was legendary Ithaca, golden Ithaca. She had a memory like an elephant's—the details of how it used to be with them, the blessed family of four.

"Last week I ordered a queen-sized pull-out couch," he replied. "When it comes you'll be able to have a friend stay over." Matina turned her head toward the train window. Phillip followed her gaze. Outside there was a highway that paralleled the tracks, a marsh, a dilapidated factory. She was silent and motionless, except for one quick searching encounter with her backpack.

"I've been wondering, does Grandma really want us to come to this concert?" Eric asked five minutes before they reached Huntstown.

"I don't think Grandma likes to ask for anything," he replied after a few moments. He saw his mother's face—careful neutrality—as though expressing a preference or a wish or *anything* was bad manners. "It doesn't matter to me," she would say with a touch of singsong and pride in her voice when someone asked her to choose something, even ice cream.

"But will it make her *happy* that we're coming?" Eric persisted.

"I don't know. I certainly hope so," Phillip said, and at that second Matina broke her silence. "We're her family. Of course she wants us to come. Of course it'll make her happy." She spoke with so much authority that Phillip believed she was right. Matina, at seventeen, was almost five years older than Eric.

"How do you *know* that Grandma Belle really wants us there?" Eric persisted, his eyes on Matina, who didn't bother to answer.

Phillip's parents had sold their substantial one-family home about seven years ago and moved into the first condominium townhouse to be built in Huntstown, the Long Island suburb where Phillip had grown up and where he and Harriet had first lived together. The afternoon concert was to be held at his old high school, an easy walk from the train station. Matina, Eric, and he strolled together, three abreast. It was warm, the middle of June, a day full of sunshine. There were wooden buckets planted with red flowers on every corner. Matina linked arms with her brother and father, and he could feel the bounce in his daughter's step. For her, until her grandfather died a year and a half ago, Huntstown stood for all that was whole and right in the world—her early years, her parents as a happy couple, her grandparents—not exactly doting but there to be counted on: everything perfect. "Huntstown heaven," Eric said with a tinge of sarcasm, because those golden years were beyond his memory, "and not one homeless person on the streets." For Phillip, Huntstown was less than idyllic: a complicated weave of history. Buying a home with Harriet and making it comfortable; the joy of having their children born there; then leaving it and his parents too abruptly to move to the South.

Once inside the high school, Phillip led his children straight to the auditorium, the school's layout indelibly imprinted on his brain: through the double doors on the right, to the end of the cor- ridor, and then a left turn. However, once he got there, he grew hesitant and stopped, turned wistful; reluctant, it seemed, to choose seats. Eric took over. He strode down the aisle and found seats for them in a row not far from the stage. The place was filling up, mainly with senior citizens, well-dressed active-looking men and women, saving seats, passing each other programs.

"You must be Belle's son, Phillip," a woman in the row behind them said, tapping him on the shoulder. "I'm Mary Sherman. Belle told me to look for you. And this must be Eric and Matina. Your mother described them to me—'Matina has a flair for fashion,' she said, 'and Eric is a handsome boy.' But wait till you see how beautiful your mother looks, Phil. Children, wait till you hear your grandmother's group."

"We're really proud of Grandma," Eric said, and Phillip shivered. His own sentiments sounded patronizing on Eric's lips.

"Ever since your dear grandfather died, your grandmother has been changing," Mrs. Sherman said, speaking to the children but looking at Phillip. "She's not so scared anymore. She's coming out of her shell. She's reaching out."

"It certainly seems that way," Phillip replied. He felt a tiny flapping of excitement as he waited to witness his mother on stage— out of her shell and transformed, a baby bird in surprisingly splendid plumage.

Matina turned to her father. "I didn't know Grandma liked to sing. Did she used to sing and dance around the house when you were young?"

Sing and dance? It had been a home where things ran smoothly but it wasn't a singing and dancing home, and of course Matina must have known that. "I never even realized that Grandma liked to sing," and to himself he said, *I never heard my mother hum one song.*

As the lights dimmed and the audience quieted, a sense of his high school years hit him, a faint memory of disappointment. He hadn't distinguished himself in any realm, disappointing himself, but more painfully several of his teachers, the ones who'd taken the trouble to get to know him, who seemed to respect him. There'd been a competition for a stage set design for the annual student musical production—that year it was *Carousel*—and his design didn't win. That was tough, but not *so* tough. What got to him was that his teacher took his talent seriously and offered him some advice: "Phil, let yourself go more. Pull out the stops." The message he received from a few of his teachers was always the same: "Don't hold back so much." But he never seemed able to let himself go, no matter how he tried. In his junior year he'd won a berth on the tennis team but by his senior year, he was kicked off for not trying hard enough. His dad was annoyed—all those tennis lessons adding up to nothing. Even with girls, some of whom he knew liked him, he couldn't overcome his self-imposed restraint. He'd hoped that the soft-skinned Lydia Berlin in her pink angora sweater would make a move toward him, seduce him, or help *him* make the first move, but she never did. This was one of the reasons he admired Matina: nothing retiring about her, he thought now as he waited for the program to start. Matina didn't hold back and secretly he relished that. There was something fierce about Matina—fiercely selfish, fiercely loyal, fiercely a royal pain in the ass. Matina seemed older than her years; she understood so much about so many things but she refused to understand that her parents' divorce was probably more her mother's decision than his, despite the fact that Harriet told her the truth.

As soon as the curtain opened the audience applauded. The choral group consisted of about twenty-two people, fifteen women and seven men. "There's Grandma," Eric whispered. "Second from the right in the first row." "That's a great dress she has on," Matina said. His mother was wearing a navy-blue dress with a sparkling white collar and bow. "Grandma has really good taste, doesn't she?" Phillip didn't respond. "Well *I* think she does," Matina insisted.

The choral group sang a selection of known and unknown music—Cole Porter, Rodgers and Hammerstein, and songs from before his time, old standbys from the twenties or thirties. The audience was in heaven and lavished their friends with frequent bursts of applause. The singers, jittery in the first couple of songs, warmed up. Their voices were sweet, but to Phillip's ear, thin; there was no resonance, no richness, and occasionally someone veered off-key. Then an elderly gentleman and a sweet-looking plump woman, who stood holding on to an aluminum walker, sang "Tea for Two." Cries of delight and more clapping. While the entire group sang "Oklahoma," Phillip's eyes settled on his mother. A certain fading had taken place in the two months since he had last seen her, a gentle wilting—small changes. She was not able to sit up straight anymore, although it was plain to see she was trying. She was trying to sit up very straight. Seventy-three years old, growing smaller. Her head jutted forward, her back curved. Almost as if to compensate, Phillip straightened his spine, pulled back his shoulders.

He continued to watch his mother. She was singing with all her heart, moving her eyes swiftly back and forth from the music on the music stand in front of her to the baton of Bob DiFranco. She was singing and reading her music, keeping one eye on Bob DiFranco. There was an expression on her face—Phillip tried to read it—of pleasure, yes, but also . . . what was it? An expression he had seen so many times but never named. His chest tightened and he turned away. It was a look he didn't want his children to see, something docile and vague, he wasn't sure. Uncomfortable, he wanted to bolt.

The heavy gray curtain closed. Along with everybody else he applauded, stopping finally when Matina stopped. Checking his program, he saw that the next segment was a series of folk dances put on by the senior citizens' dance group, followed by a ten-minute intermission, followed by the final offering of the choral group. In the dark minute between acts, while Eric was whispering his approval of his grandmother's performance, Phillip suppressed a yawn. Just then Mrs. Sherman touched his shoulder. "I want you to be sure to notice the beautiful dancer you're about to see: Helena Whiteley. Eighty-two years old. And don't tell me I'm lying—she *is* eighty-two."

Phillip worried that he wouldn't be able to tell Helena Whiteley from the other women on the stage. He also worried that the folk dances, usually danced by lusty youth, would seem ludicrous when performed by cautious golden-agers. Something about being in this auditorium made him worry about everything. Indeed, when the curtain parted, he could see that the men on the stage were frail. One man in yellow plaid trousers kept heading in the wrong direction when it was his turn to promenade his partner, and his partner had to yank him around, tactfully of course, in the opposite direction. However, it was not difficult to tell who Helena Whiteley was. She was the tall woman with soft, white hair piled high on her head, and a straight supple body. She was dancing, not performing, not pretending. Phillip could feel his whole body unwind as he gave in to watching only Helena Whiteley. He was being unfair, he thought. Each dancer deserved equal attention—each person was trying, each person was brave—but his gaze always returned to that woman, and as it did the muscles in his legs relaxed, although minutes before he hadn't known they were tense.

Matina whispered, "I don't believe she's eighty-two." And a voice from behind them, Mrs. Sherman's, piped up. "She is. I saw her passport last year."

Helena Whiteley was dressed in a flowing, pale blue flowered skirt and a white blouse edged with blue embroidery that looked eastern European. There was a white fabric belt around her waist. Good God she actually had a waist. She had hips. Her breasts were round and high and quite separate from her midriff. She wore beige high-heeled shoes with narrow straps—the kind that dancers wear; "character shoes"—he recalled the name for them. Each step she took mattered. There was nothing shuffling about the way she moved her feet. Her legs were shapely.

"I don't believe she's eighty-two," Eric murmured.

Helena Whiteley managed the English folk dances with spirit, but she was especially fluid and stately in the Greek dance known as *Misalu*. She shifted directions with one clean, flowing movement. Eric, who had started taking ballet classes four months ago, kept his eyes on the woman, and made a low whistling sound each time she made a good, sharp shift of direction. A section of her soft white hair came unpinned and a few locks swiped across her forehead, making her look, Phillip thought, almost youthful. She held her head with a pride that stopped an inch away from arrogance.

"She does yoga," Mrs. Sherman, leaning forward, whispered in his ear.

An almost inadmissable longing occurred to Phillip—to have a mother who could dance like Helena Whiteley, to have a mother who did yoga.

In the final dance, a dance from Hungary, Helena Whiteley put one hand on her hip, the other in the air and moved it as though she were waving hello. Several people in the audience broke into applause, and Phillip was sure that it was in response to the lovely openness of Helena's gesture, which she alone had added to the dance. He found himself applauding, too, and Eric, transfixed, couldn't stop clapping. "She's awesome," he whispered.

There was a clearly discernible mumble in the audience about Helena Whiteley during intermission. Phillip heard it all around him. It had mostly to do with disbelief about her age. Mrs. Sherman and Matina were also discussing it. Eric chirped, "I don't think she even looks *seventy*."

"How do you know what a seventy-year-old woman looks like?" Matina challenged, and Eric shrugged. "*I* know."

"It's not a matter of age—age is never that important," Phillip said to Matina and Eric when Mrs. Sherman turned away to talk to her friends; "what's important is that Helena Whiteley knows who she is. I mean, I don't know her, but to me she seems to have a sense"—he hesitated—"of what's right for herself." He suddenly realized that his intensity made him open to ridicule.

"How can you tell so much from watching a woman do a few folk dances for twenty minutes!" Matina went on almost angrily. She had slipped out of her pink plastic shoes and was hugging her zebra-striped knees. "You're *imagining* what she's like."

"I don't think I am," he replied confidently.

"Of course you are. You're coloring in the lines. You have no idea what Helena Whiteley is really like."

· Eric changed the subject. "I kept worrying that Grandma would goof, but she didn't. Grandma's singing group was great."

Phillip agreed.

"But what didn't you like about the way Grandma looked?" Matina pressed.

"Who said I didn't like the way Grandma looked?"

Matina insisted that she could tell and pushed him to explain, but he demurred. "I don't think you like the tailored look," Matina said after a while. "I guess I didn't care for the little white bow," Phillip finally admitted, and then regretted that his daughter had gotten him to say anything at all.

The second part of the choral group's program began with a presentation of flowers to Bob DiFranco, the young conductor, by one of the men in the group. The choral leader's energy and patience and good cheer were praised to the sky. Bob DiFranco bowed modestly to the audience, who bathed him in affectionate glances and applause. DiFranco was perhaps twenty-five or twenty-six, small and lithe with dark curly hair. Phillip knew that his mother was one of Bob DiFranco's most ardent fans. "His smile is a tonic for all of us," she had told him a month ago on the phone. "We'd do anything for that nice young man." At the time he had felt a silly little rumble of jealousy for Bob DiFranco. Now his mother applauded until the moment Bob lifted his arm and gave the signal to begin singing. He noticed then that his mother had dyed her hair the same color as Matina's, pale blond.

He listened to the medley of old favorites, "Down in the Valley," "You Are My Sunshine," and saw delight written on his mother's face. It occurred to him that she was a woman who always took pride in not wanting anything she didn't have, not asking for anything. Not wanting anything was what she believed made her lovable. But it had, for him at least, made her harder to love because he'd come to feel over the years that he never knew what he could do to please her. The only time he was certain he'd made her happy was when he and Harriet bought their home in Huntstown. That decision had soothed a lot of ruffled feelings.

He watched her closely, her hands folded in her lap, her hands as white as moonlight against the navy blue of her dress. Her eyes did their dance, moving quickly from the music on the stand in front of her to the figure of Bob DiFranco and back to the music.

She had wanted to join this group, and had. That was impressive. He gave her credit, and yet as he did he allowed himself to imagine being the other woman's—Helena Whiteley's—son. What sort of a man would he have been? Would he have been bolder? More determined? More abandoned? He saw himself on the beach with a group of friends—men and women, building sand castles with ingenious turrets and towers and domes, a Kremlin-like compound. Suntanned, agile, he was bouncing around on the sand, laughing, speaking foreign languages, wearing a straw hat. Everyone was wearing a shade hat of some sort. Women were enchanted by his playfulness and flirted with him, and he could tell simply by looking at them which language each woman spoke. As soon as he felt Matina's eyes on him, he stopped daydreaming and went back to watching his mother. For a split second he saw her lose her place in the music, look worried and frantic, then glance quickly at DiFranco and find her place again.

What was the expression on her face that had made him want to flee the auditorium earlier in the concert? It came to him now. Obedience. She was obedient. As though his mother was in class and trying to be good, waiting for what the teacher wanted her to do next. Phillip twisted anxiously in his seat, unfolding his legs, then folding them again. His program slid off his lap.

When the concert ended there was a rush for the front of the auditorium. The singers were filing offstage. Some of them were already waving to their families and friends, and calling out to them. He watched his mother remove loose pages of music from her music stand and tap them into a neat pile.

He could barely move. Eric and Matina stood up. "That was excellent," Eric said. "They were good." "Grandma looked so happy," Matina exclaimed. "I don't think I've ever seen her look so *blissed out*—even when Grandpa was alive and you and Mom were together." Matina glanced at her father, waiting for a response. "Yes, she was having a great time," he said with some difficulty.

His daughter was looking at him strangely. "What didn't you like about it, Dad?" she asked.

"I didn't say anything about not liking it." He paused, faltering for a second. "I loved it," he said emphatically.

Matina's face lost its ruddy color, grew clouded. "You didn't love it." She stared at him for a moment or two, then turned away and was sidestepping her way out of the row. He could see only the back of her head, her painfully short, dyed-yellow hair. But he knew exactly what she was thinking: that he was a liar, and more than that—that he was a traitor.

Matina moved ahead, didn't glance around at him again. The distance she created in her wake was dry scorched earth. Both children clutched their concert programs in their hands. Eric was ahead of his sister, hurrying toward the stage, toward his grandmother, with his head held high, grazing the sky, and his young dancer's posture. His eyes were focused, his arms outstretched as though his whole body was about to leap and lift off over the heads of the audience and land him in his grandmother's lap. His son was growing taller, his shoulders broadening out. A noisy buzz rose up around Phillip in the auditorium. He leaned down and tried to find his program under their seats, and couldn't. Then, out of the corner of his eye, he observed Matina slip two programs into her red-and-lavender backpack. She was building her case against him.

He took off after her. He had absolutely no idea of what to say. What could he say? Within seconds he was tapping her shoulder, stretching out his arm. "I'd like my program back, please."

She pulled back, stared at him. "You threw it on the floor."

"You picked it up."

"You didn't like the concert," she shot back.

He stared at her, at a loss for what to say.

"You were sitting there picking everything and everyone apart, including Grandma. Everyone except that woman, that show-off who thought she was God's gift to dancing. You were madly in love with that woman." She stopped, then murmured, "Poor Grandma."

Once again Phillip was tempted to explain why Helena White-ley captivated him. He took a deep breath as though he were about to take a high dive into cold green water, and explain yet again what he so respected about the woman. *Shut up about Helena Whiteley*, he told himself, and aloud to Matina, he said, "You have my program." His voice was even, controlled.

His daughter stared at him blankly, then gazed beyond his right shoulder toward the stage. For once she was at a loss for words as though suddenly she had forgotten why she was so angry with him. For a few seconds there were no answers, no questions taking shape, no questions spiraling and arching, ballooning. No words at all. She looked confused and young, her eyes tearing slightly, her hair pathetically shorn.

While he waited, his eyes scanned the stage. He saw that Eric had reached his grandmother, and when he tried to embrace her, she offered him a dry cheek, a quick little peck. Phillip swallowed, and turning back to his daughter, he held out his hand.

Her gray eyes storming, she refused to return the program. It wasn't easy for him to stand there, each heartbeat drumming in his ears, *Give in, give in.* He loved her so much. "I'd like my program, please," he said; and he waited patiently. Finally she put the program in his hand. The paper felt as light as a butterfly. He folded it and slipped it in his pocket. "Grandma is waiting for us," he said. "Come on."

On the stage his mother, her cheeks flushed, her body leaning toward them, was waving. Phillip waved back.

Woman Made of Sand

Marianne began to jog in the mornings with Eric, her husband's son. She liked Eric's company and the way he ran. He was a careful runner; his feet were precious to him. He wore expensive running shoes—dove gray—and spotless white cotton socks. Their route took them past Blake Pond where Eric and his older sister, Matina, swam in the late afternoons.

Marianne knew that Phillip was still sleeping. She knew that Matina was still sleeping. That's practically all Matina did—except of course to go to Blake Pond with Eric—before dinner. Convenient timing.

Phillip deserved to sleep. He was "bone tired," he had told friends in the city before they set out for the Cape. She had found the expression more embarrassing each time he used it. Couldn't he simply tell people he was tired? Also, it bothered her that she hadn't seen the signs of such exhaustion. Looking back, she wasn't sure whether there had been any signs to see.

Eric, his pace more uneven than hers, ran alongside her. "It must be strange," she said to him, "to spend so much time with women. You're surrounded by a million adorable ballerinas."

"It's no problem." The boy seemed to shrug while he ran. He was serious, had missed the humor in her observation. "The real problem is putting all my eggs in one basket. Ballet is the beginning and end of my life," he explained. "I don't get to do anything but practice and rehearse and take class. My brain is shrinking. It's shriveling up like one of those dried black mushrooms Dad puts into everything he cooks."

Of course he would get tired of doing the same thing day in and day out, year after year. Even on vacation he was chained to a regimen of keeping in shape. He did an hour and a quarter of barre work, using the porch railing on the back of their rented house, every evening. His discipline made him seem older than seventeen. Marianne admired that discipline.

"You seem to have a good life, though," she said after a few minutes. "More interesting than most seventeen-year-olds."

"I agree," Eric said quickly. He broke his stride and did a *grand jeté*, and she laughed.

For about a mile they ran on a downgrade. The air smelled of pine woods and sea salt. She felt sorry for Phillip because Eric was often short-tempered and condescending to him. Everything Phillip said the boy either contradicted or corrected. If Phillip said Iraq, Eric said Iran. If Phillip said Guadalajara, Eric said Guatemala. Phillip told Marianne he didn't care—it was normal "oedipal stuff"—he was simply happy that Eric treated Marianne with respect. "He treats me warmly," Marianne said, and then worried for an instant that *she* had corrected Phillip.

"We have something in common," Eric said, catching up with her again, his gray T-shirt stained with sweat.

"What's that?"

"We both seem to like punishing our bodies."

The remark hit Marianne like an icy snowball. "I run because it feels good," she replied a moment later. And after a while, she added, "I've been running for years; even before I met your father."

Matina and Phillip were having coffee at an oval table they had moved from the living room to the back porch. They were sitting on orange canvas chairs, and Matina was wearing jeans and a bathing suit top. She was explaining something to her father, using her beautifully shaped hands, cutting at the air as though she were demonstrating surgical incisions. At twenty-two she was going into her second year of medical school and helped support herself by modeling occasionally at fashion shows for big-name designers. If she ever put on too much weight for modeling clothes, she had once told Marianne, she could model rings and bracelets. She had the hands for it. She had the hands for diamonds and emeralds, she had once said. She stopped talking to her father when Marianne approached. Phillip stood up to give Marianne his chair and went into the kitchen to get another one for himself.

"Did you find the croissants?" Marianne asked Matina. Matina nodded. Both women had been amused that Phillip had bought dozens of croissants in the city and brought them along frozen, wrapped in an old Sunday *Times*. Almond croissants were his latest addiction. Phillip was the focus of all their attention. He was the hub of the wheel.

Phillip returned to the table, bringing the reheated coffee and a croissant for Marianne. He stood behind her and let his hand rest on her shoulder, close to her neck. His hand said *love* in a secret sign language that she could feel but that Matina couldn't see.

"Did Dad tell you I'm flying to Milan at the end of the month to do a couple of shows for Silvio Torelli?" Matina asked. "I'm going to meet Mom there for a week's vacation after the shows." Marianne shook her head.

"When do you have to be back in school?" Phillip asked.

"I'm not exactly sure. September twelfth, I think." The conversation fizzled, as it often did when Matina referred to her mother, something she did as much as possible. It was a relief to hear Eric singing and humming upstairs. He was finished with his shower. "He must be dancing in *Petrouchka*," Matina said; "I hear Stravinsky."

Marianne left the porch to take her turn in the shower. She was sure that the music that Eric had been humming upstairs was not Stravinsky but Prokofiev.

Around noon they went to the beach. Eric walked ahead, carrying four small chairs. Marianne admired his posture and build. A year ago when one of her caseworker friends from the social service agency where she worked asked him if he lifted weights, he had answered, "No, I lift girls." He liked to talk about his *pas de deux* class—learning "how to partner."

"It's quite an art," he said; "you have to be very sensitive. You have to be dependable." He prayed for the petite ballerinas and joked occasionally about the horses who strained his back when he had to lift them off the ground. But even in his joking he was kind. Some of the best dancers fell into the horse category. They couldn't help it if they were on the large side.

When they reached their usual spot on the beach, Eric threw the chairs down and ran toward the water. "Hey Matina, a giant jellyfish! Come look." He picked up the gelatinous mess and waved it. "Wait a minute," Matina said, unzipping her jeans. "You're always so hyper."

Marianne and Phillip set up their encampment—each person's books in a separate pile, the lunch basket in a small patch of shade behind the chairs. "These vacations aren't easy on you," Phillip said, unrolling two bamboo mats. "Matina basically ignores you."

"A small penalty," Marianne said. She put her hand on Phillip's cheek; he had squatted down next to her chair. "It's not the way she treats me," Marianne said slowly. "It's that Matina's become so confident. She gets what she wants. One good thing leads to another." It had struck her these past few days that Matina seemed to be growing larger and larger and that she was shrinking.

A shadow passed over Phillip's face. "I think you should stop running."

"The doctor said it was okay."

"Even so."

Marianne stiffened. "You're probably right," she said.

Eric and Matina tried to wave Phillip into the water, but Marianne could tell that he didn't want to leave her alone right then. Closing his eyes, he leaned back in the chair next to hers. He's bone-tired, Marianne said to herself, but as she silently said those words she was watching Matina, who was wading up to her knees in the surf. Matina had lost the emaciated appearance of the past few years, and was adding weight to hips and bust. The weight was actually flattering but she might really have to switch from high fashion to jewelry, and then she would lose out on her jaunts to Paris and Milan.

In one swift movement Matina dove into an oncoming wave; Eric followed. She remembered first meeting Matina and Eric four years ago when she was twenty-five. Matina and Eric had not been *wunderkind* then. Eric, even though he was studying ballet, was a klutz, and Matina was neither brilliant nor beautiful. She

was an ordinary college student, furious at her father for finding a
new woman to love. She seemed to hate Marianne, but when
either of them suggested as much, Matina denied it. The only person she was angry at was her Barnard history professor who had not
appreciated her paper on Bismarck, and had given her a B-plus
instead of an A-plus. Marianne asked to read the paper, and ended
up agreeing with Matina. In those days Marianne was able to be
exquisitely fair.

Phillip opened his eyes, reached for the thermos behind his
chair, and poured Marianne a cup of iced tea. He had made beautiful sandwiches for them all and packed them in the wicker picnic basket his mother had given them, a gift Belle had received
from a cousin in England years before and never used. Phil liked
that basket.

Marianne sipped the iced tea. "Something's been bothering
me," she said: "that you told the Mintons and Ellie that you were
'bone tired.' I didn't realize that you were *that* tired."

"I wasn't *that* tired."

"But you used that expression—'bone tired.'"

"It's just an expression," Phil said.

"Maybe I'm being overly sensitive."

"I won't say it again," Phillip promised. "But—I wish you'd stop
running."

"The discipline means a lot."

"You're not an undisciplined person, sweetie."

"My work is with people," Marianne explained. "The accom-
plishments are always ambiguous. Running is clear-cut."

"But I still wish you'd stop."

Marianne stood up. "Is walking okay?"

The beach was walkable for miles in either direction. A sand cliff formed a steep wall parallel to the water. It was as though the ocean, fierce and hungry, had rolled in one night and taken an enormous bite out of the land. And yet, there were no signs of violence: soft lines, nothing jagged or sharp. In places, sand sifted down the side of the cliff leaving gentler slopes; beach heather grew in thick clumps.

Marianne and Phillip held hands. The tide was out. Bits of sea life littered the water's edge. It was only moments before Matina and Eric caught up with them, and all four walked along together. These walks were their one family ritual. Four years of walking along this shore, picking up razor clams, starfish, shells, and stones. Matina knew the Latin names for almost all the shells; she recognized the fiddler crab and the blue crab and the horseshoe crab. She could distinguish among seaweeds: knew which was dulse and which was kelp and which was sea lettuce. Matina was a walking encyclopedia; she had endless amounts of information at her fingertips. Was it possible that her mother, Harriet, or Phillip, or both of them at some point years past, in the other life, had taught her all the names for everything, all the music, all the famous people, all the important dates, all the wildflowers and trees?

Suddenly Eric threw his collection of shells into the water, ran ahead twenty yards, leaped and jumped, pirouetted, did his amazing (to him) *double tours*, one "almost-perfect" *triple tours*. Marianne loved watching him. He was becoming a dancer. She wanted to see him in an entire finished performance, with music and costumes and scenery.

Phillip was not watching Eric; he was picking up every mussel shell on the beach. For a few moments the little group lost its unity. Marianne waited for Eric, finally asking him whether he was rehearsing *Petrouchka*. He nodded. "How'd you know?"

"We heard you humming it in the bathroom this morning," she replied, furious that Matina had been right: it was Stravinsky.

Back at their chairs, Phillip dumped an armload of mussels and stones and pieces of shell onto his towel.

"Those aren't very pretty," Eric said to his father.

"I know that."

"What are they for?"

"Be patient."

"I can't. I don't have your patience," Eric said.

The father was patient, Marianne thought; sometimes too patient.

"How about helping me?" Phillip said to his son. "Get a heavy stone and start breaking shells into small pieces."

Eric and Phillip pulled the towel with all the shells closer to the water. On his hands and knees, Phillip heaped sand together, patting it into a hill. He worked with concentration. From her chair, Marianne deciphered a rural landscape with hills and valleys and roadways. Whatever it was, Phillip seemed busy, lively, not bone tired. It was she who felt tired—tired of trying, tired of working at things that shouldn't require work. All she wanted was to have a baby, then have another; to be at the heart of her own small family. She closed her eyes but couldn't doze. Instead of trying to sleep, she watched Phillip. He was working with intensity now. No, he was playing in the sand like a child; what he needed was a little red pail and shovel. Eric wasn't around.

"Did Eric go back to the house?" Marianne asked Phillip. Unable to resist seeing what Phillip was making from closer range, she had risen and moved closer to him. Marianne had to repeat the question. "He's searching for white stones," Phillip finally said, and when Marianne asked what for, Phillip smiled mysteriously and raised his eyebrows. "You'll see."

His secrecy, his playfulness annoyed her. "Phillip, what are you making?"

"I don't know." He didn't look up.

"Dad's always wanted to make things," Matina informed her. "He's never really liked the wallpaper business. He went into it because Grandpa Roger needed him, but he never loved it." Matina's entire body was greased with suntan lotion. Half the plastic jar was gone in one application. She turned to her father, who was kneeling in the sand. "It's too bad, Dad, that you can't take some time off and get into doing art." For a moment Phillip looked as if he'd been slapped in the face.

Eric appeared and dropped a bunch of small white stones in the sand. Turning to Marianne, he said, "Let's run earlier tomorrow morning. How about 6:45?"

"I probably won't run tomorrow morning."

"You're not preggers, are you?" Eric asked.

Deeply embarrassed, she shook her head no.

"You're making a woman," Marianne said to Phillip, who had finished the rough figure and was now putting detail on the face: shaping a nose and cheekbones, building up a mouth. He covered the forehead with chips of blue mussel shell.

"Who is she?" Marianne asked. The figure was too broad to be her, the breasts and hips too large. Phillip didn't reply. He was working on the legs, which at first hadn't been defined; she'd thought he was making a mermaid. She walked to the water, and returned. "Do you want lunch?" "Not yet," Phillip said.

"Looks like Mom," Matina said, staring at her father's sculpture. He was padding the hips with more sand.

"Mom!" Phillip was surprised.

"Mom—Harriet, the woman you used to be married to; our mother."

"It's not Mom," Phillip said firmly.

Relieved, Marianne entered the water. It was cold. She floated on her back for a few moments. She was thinking about Phillip and herself: that they had never wanted sacrifice or martyrdom to be part of their relationship; they had wanted generosity. They didn't want a marriage of quibbling and negotiation and bookkeeping. No list-keeping for them, no punctilious mathematical sharing of money or chores. If they had a child, she'd be happy to take care of it. She turned over and swam a few strokes. Without running she might have to take swimming more seriously. Only once had Phillip let out his frustrations with their efforts to conceive. "I don't look forward to temperature charts or making love on a schedule."

"Do you think I do?" she'd shouted. Guilty later, she wanted to apologize for her outburst but found that she couldn't.

The bedrock of their relationship was kindness and careful attention. They had met at a benefit performance of *The Nut-cracker* to raise money for El Salvadoran orphans. Eric was dancing in the corps of children and Marianne's friend, Elena, was one of his ballet teachers. Later, at the reception, Elena introduced them. They discovered that each of them had been put off by the opulence of the reception and the presence of so many celebrities— Baryshnikov and Twyla Tharp and Jerome Robbins and others—

convinced that the honorable thing to do was to adopt an El Salvadoran child and not go to events like this one.

Chilled, Marianne made her way out of the water. Phillip
didn't notice her. He was redoing the stomach, accentuating the
pelvic bones and rounding out the tummy. He was setting white
stones in a circular pattern on the stomach.

"Why don't you use a starfish for a belly button," Matina suggested, and then insisted that the figure *was* Harriet. "It's mom
when she was pregnant."

"I don't think it's Mom," Eric said. "It's too sexy."

"Mom is sexy," Matina said. Phillip was untangling skeins of seaweed. He was oblivious to everyone.

Although Marianne didn't want to watch Phillip, she couldn't
stop. Something about the sand figure repulsed her. It was a large-
hipped, full-breasted woman, and she was a slim, tiny woman, a
woman who never had to worry about gaining weight. Phillip had
appreciated that. Harriet, from what Phillip had told her, was
always on diets, some of which she imposed on the family with
varying rationales. Now staring at the sand lady, Marianne had two
questions: did Phillip really like her thinness; had Harriet ever had
trouble conceiving?

"I'm going back to the house," Eric stated. "I've had enough of
Dad's sex goddess."

"You're acting like an asshole," Matina told Eric and then
turned to her father. "The clavicle's set a little too low."

"I don't need an anatomy lesson," Phillip said. "Will you please
back off."

"I can't believe you don't recognize Mom," Matina said. "Even the
feet—the way the toes get smaller in equal increments like steps."

"You mean 'phalanges,'" Eric said.

"How do you know that?" Matina laughed, impressed.

"A dancer knows the bones of the foot. Feet are to the dancer as hands are to the surgeon."

"You're a smart little bro." Matina hugged Eric. She was taller than he.

"Will you two get the hell out of here!" Phillip said to his children. He was inlaying shells in the arms.

"Give your father some peace," Marianne said. She was startled by Phillip's temper—and also felt angry, but not at the kids, at Phillip.

"It's too much how you pamper each other," Matina said to Marianne, loud enough for Phillip to hear.

"Can't you leave me alone!" Phillip muttered, leaping to his feet and facing his children. Then he regained control, twisted away from them, spiraled down onto the sand. Matina and Eric retreated.

"To tell the truth, I'm glad to see you lose your patience," Matina said. Phillip raised his eyebrows, wanted to say something but didn't. Marianne wished he could get mad at Matina but he scarcely ever did. For a few seconds no one said anything; then Matina and Eric took off for Blake Pond, leaving all their belongings except for their towels. Marianne knew that she and Phillip would probably have to trudge up the hill with the extra load.

With Eric and Matina gone, Phillip went back to work on his sculpture. He was silent, remote. It seemed reasonable that sometimes Phillip needed to remove himself from his children's demands, but now they were gone. She waited for him to smile at her, say something, touch her. He continued to work on his woman. Slowly the tide was edging in, a wavering line of foamy water licking the sand. He didn't seem to notice—neither the tide, nor her. He looked silly, she thought. She didn't like watching him—jumping up and darting down the beach to find more shells, more gobs of seaweed, running back and kneeling down. He maneuvered around the figure in jerky bounces on his knees. A pie-faced toddler in a soggy Pampers came over to inspect. Phillip didn't smile at her. She handed him a stone. He thanked her. The child watched him for a few minutes, and walked away.

The sun dipped behind the sand cliff, the air temperature cooled. Marianne reached for Phillip's denim shirt. The ocean was rolling in a few inches further with every breaking wave. She could no longer bear to watch him. Phillip reminded her of the autistic children she had worked with on her first social work job— pleased, it almost seemed, that their terrible inscrutability protected them from doing what other people wanted them to do. Watching Phillip, she half-imagined she heard little clucking sounds. He was in the center of his own world, in possession of his perfect woman. He was in possession of everything he wanted. He had his family, his own children. He didn't need their baby. Did he need her? Her gaze reached out over the ocean to a tanker far away on the horizon line; the tanker was as gray as fog. Unspeakable anger filled her. A longing to get even. She was not going to give up running. She ran before she had ever met Phillip. Her doctor said it was okay to run, and she would listen to her doctor.

Marianne gathered their belongings, organized them, piled up the chairs. "Phillip, it's time to go."

"A few more minutes."

"The tide is going to cover Wonder Woman in a few minutes. I'm going back now."

"I'm almost finished."

"I'd rather not wait," Marianne said.

"Do you have your camera with you?" he asked.

She shook her head no.

Phillip stood up and took a few steps away from his sculpture. He was smiling. "She's really lovely," he pronounced, squinting and gazing down at the figure. "I had such a good time this afternoon." Marianne was quiet but Phillip didn't seem to notice. "It felt like the ocean was inside of me—the waves and swells and currents—even the sparkle." He moved around to the other side of the sand woman and repositioned a few white stones in the stomach area. "I like how she turned out," he said.

The more Phillip liked his sand woman, the more Marianne hated her. She wanted to walk over her, through her; she wanted to kick up sand and trample her, destroy her. Of course Phillip loved his nice little lady: she needed nothing from him; she was silent and docile and complete.

Marianne folded two of the chairs that Eric had carried down to the beach, leaving the other two for Phillip. She loaded herself down with as much of their belongings as she could. She was a small, thin beast of burden, and as she climbed the hill, she wondered if she and Phillip were having their first real fight. What frightened her was that she didn't know what it was about. It was about nothing—and everything, as enormous as the ocean in front of her. It was about the fact that he had already lived the life she longed for. The only thought that consoled her was that within thirty minutes the tide would take the woman away. In less than an hour there would be no trace of her.

Madonna at Monterchi

om!" someone screamed outside the baggage claims area of the Milan Airport. I turned and saw my daughter with her thick hair pulled back and tied in a blue silk scarf, wearing a pair of jeans and a loose polo shirt that had *Coney Island* written in large faded red letters. As I watched her make her way toward me, the skin of my body craved the softness of hers. Crazy reaction: Matina's twenty-two years old and she'd been in Milan for a week doing fashion shows for the Milanese designer, Silvio Torelli. I hadn't seen her since June and it was now the beginning of September.

"Ma!" she screamed, scooting over to my side. She carried a khaki army shoulder bag and up close I could see she was disheveled, even a little dirty-looking—not like a fashion model or a second-year medical student, both of which she was. I had pictured her sleek and well groomed in a new Torelli outfit. In the moment it took for me to appraise her appearance, she had me locked in a powerful embrace.

"What's the matter, darling?" I asked instinctively.

"It's good to see you."

We hugged again, and this time I noticed that Matina had her suitcase with her. I was surprised because we'd planned to spend the night in Milan at her hotel and not leave till the following day for a week's vacation together in Florence and Tuscany. Sensing my confusion, Matina explained that she called the *pensione* in Florence to ask if our room might be available for tonight. It was, and they promised to hold it for us. "Ma, Signora Riccelli sounded so sweet," she added.

"Matina," I said impatiently, "I didn't sleep a wink on the plane. I'm exhausted."

She apologized for the change of plans and justified them. She had to get out of Milan; the shows were exhausting and she was never going to do them again—not in Milan, not in Paris, not in New York, not in Dallas or anywhere else. Moreover, she hated Silvio's new line: skimpy tight coats and jackets in garish colors, like chartreuse and blood red or mustard yellow or screaming parrot blue. Vulgar colors whereas all the other designers were working with earth tones, even with black. Black was wonderful. Black was flattering. The angry edge to her voice was unfamiliar. The fashion scene had always provided Matina with a supply of amusing behind-the-scene happenings and mishaps that she dramatized for any willing audience. I liked that glimpse into a world far from my own. I work for the State of New Jersey, in their Department of Environmental Protection, Division of Solid Waste Management; in other words—garbage. The industrial world is inundated with garbage. It's fascinating work, important work, but it's rarely amusing.

"Matina, something's the matter. "What is it?" I had my own

nervous little scenarios about modeling, centering on drugs and sexploitation, a corrupt superficial world that consumed young women and spit them out used up, brokenhearted, emaciated, and cocaine-addicted. She assured me that nothing was wrong and led me to the car rental place where she had made arrangements to pick up our Fiat. She would drive so that I could sleep.

In Florence I fell in love with the Pensione Riccelli, which occupied the fourth floor of a five-story building along the Arno, and with the Ricellis, that elderly refined trio, a married couple and a sister—although I couldn't tell who was married to whom. The three of them spoke to each other in gentle whispers, and handed each other things—a letter, a pen, a cup of tea, the telephone receiver—with so much tenderness. The price of all this atmosphere and gentility was unbelievably reasonable.

Five minutes after we inspected our high-ceilinged room, Matina unzipped her jeans, stepped out of them, and crashed down on one of the twin beds, asleep within moments. I opened the window and leaned out. I could see the river and the Ponte Vecchio, a lovelier sight than I'd ever imagined. For a long time I watched the river, yellowish and fast moving. As evening traffic increased, the air coming through the window turned acrid. There were obviously no regulations that limited motor vehicle emissions in the greater Florence area. New Jersey was way ahead on that score.

Matina awoke about a half-hour later, shifted herself to the edge of the bed, sat there numbly for a few seconds unable to decide, I thought, whether she was hungry or not. I put on a new cotton dress and finally she pulled on her same old jeans. "You don't want to wear something nicer?" I asked. "These are fine," she said gruffly. A few minutes later on our way out, we passed Signor Riccelli, with his patient eyes. "Enjoy your dinner," he called after us.

It was a summery night and we ate outdoors at a small restaurant on the busy Piazza della Signoria—and Matina made quick, decisive choices from the menu, which was a relief to me. Ever since high school, since her father's and my divorce, she had almost anorectic eating habits. Tonight she ordered well: sole and *piselli alla Fiorentina*, and finished it all. I ordered the same.

The evening dissolved—with strolling and being benevolently stared at by men (because of Matina, I assumed) and watching a performance of four sinewy young mimes in a corner of the piazza and a long-haired flamethrower in another part, and having gelato, and gaping at stylish Italian shoes in store windows. When we passed one particularly lovey-dovey young couple I asked Matina if she wished she were still with Adam, the young man she had lived with for over a year until a couple of months ago. "*You* miss Adam, I don't," she told me, and I thought she might be right about that: I was very fond of him, of his jolliness. In my opinion young women don't appreciate cheerfulness. They want some wretched, despondent fellow who they can woo into happiness with all their charms and wiles, with all that overrated talent for empathy.

Matina resented my bringing up Adam. "Ten years from now, or even twenty," she said bitterly, "you'll remember Adam and you'll think I should have stayed with him." I apologized but then inadvertently fanned the fires by acknowledging how much I trusted him. He was one of those people who could see wonderful possibilities in everything, like a cartoonist who takes a pen line squiggle and makes wildly fanciful creatures out of it. She accused me of being unfairly critical of her and her judgment. "I always supported you when you decided to leave Dad—and afterward when you had your doubts." She started to cry, which struck me as unusual for Matina, who was not a crier. "Yes, you have," I said seriously, appreciatively.

"Ma," she cried, hugging me. I patted her back, happy to be holding her again. Then she began to giggle. I asked what was so funny, and she couldn't quite explain it—something about acting very Italian. I could literally feel her anger dissipate into the damp night air—we were near the river now—and her humor return.

"Mother, we're basically so different!" she exclaimed a few moments later.

"We are?" I hadn't been aware of the fact that we were *that* different. To be honest, I thought we had a lot in common.

We made our way back toward our pensione on the less trafficky side of the Arno, warning each other about and then dodging or jumping over huge mounds of dogshit, speculating on whether there existed an especially productive breed of Florentine dog, and generally feeling happy. We were both looking forward to a couple of days of sightseeing before taking off for the countryside. Matina put her arm around my shoulder and admitted that she did occasionally miss Adam. I felt a shiver of relief. I often worried that whether she knew it or not, having lived through her father's and my divorce, Matina was wary of love.

Over breakfast the next morning in the high-ceilinged dining room, biting into a crusty roll, Matina made some offhand comments about her weight. She'd eaten too heartily on vacation in August with her father, she explained; and Marianne, her father's wife, and her brother, Eric, talked about food all day and packed

gourmet picnic lunches for the beach, but she was sure that the
added poundage would fall away once she was back racing from
lab to lab, from lab to ward to lecture hall. I was pleased with how
sensible she sounded and attributed it to her beginning identifica-
tion with the world of physicians and health care. How thrilled she
was with medicine and the science of healing! How she was
champing at the bit to save lives! To heal the wounds of
humankind! I had it in mind to tell her that she looked beautiful,
but I held back.

"Mother, you're so quiet. What's up?"

She caught me off guard. "I was thinking how beautiful you
look."

"I look disgusting!" she countered with vehemence. "Everyone
in Milan thought I looked sloppy—even Torelli. One vile pea
green coat I had to wear open because I couldn't close the buttons
across the bust." Matina's voice flared and other guests in the dining room turned to look at us. I told her to pipe down, that she was
acting like a teenager. Matina touched my hand. "I'm sorry," she
said, "it doesn't matter that much. Modeling doesn't make sense
anymore—I have no time for it. I could have been working on the
blood-pressure mobile in Staten Island for the past two weeks if I
didn't have this stupid commitment to Silvio."

"It's time to get out of it, then," I said, agreeing.

She stared at me blankly.

There were moments in the next couple of days when I felt a perfect connection with my daughter and with jewel-like Florence, a
city which is both strangely austere and outrageously glutted with
art and sights and history. Matina had taken a course in Renais-

sance painting in college and insisted on going to places that might not have seemed absolutely necessary to me. We had to see every Fra Angelico fresco in every monk's cell in the convent at San Marco, and almost every one was exquisite. Interesting details about the artists' lives popped out of Matina's memory. She knew, for instance, that Fra Angelico always said a prayer when he took up his brushes to begin painting each morning, and that he wept whenever he painted Christ on the cross. I liked nothing better than listening to her explain the different schools of painting, "lineages," almost like the biblical "begats": Piero della Francesco begat the artist Perugino who begat the great Raphael. The pleasure of having my world broadened by my daughter's knowledge made me forgive her occasional lapses into complaining.

On our third and last morning in Florence I urged Matina back to the Uffizi Gallery because there were paintings I wanted to see again. They were the luminous paintings of the Madonna with her milky radiance—the ones of the Annunciation, and of Madonna and Child, and of the Adoration with the three kings, and the Virgin admiring the infant Christ. Although my father's family was Catholic, he was not a believer, but now I felt how inspired the Church had been to call forth the power of the Mother and of human birth itself. I tried to tell Matina how much of life's sweetness and hopefulness I could feel in those paintings. "There's both a sense of serene completeness and life force," I said, pointing to one of the Madonna and child paintings. Matina seemed vaguely receptive—she didn't shoot down my theories immediately, but after a while she said, "I wish there were other ways to show female energy; perhaps women in nature—women on horseback, women on the rough seas, women on the craggy peaks of mountains . . ." Her voice trailed off. She was tired of pushing through the

crowded galleries, tired of art, tired of my theories. As we hit the
glary sunlight outside in the piazza, Matina turned to me and
said—and now she sounded huffy—"Georgia O'Keeffe gets a lot of
mileage out of her flower paintings. That's female imagery. . . ."
"Without the female," I said, and she ended the conversation by
accusing me of narrow vision, and then she announced that she
was hungry. We made our way across the Ponte Vecchio to find a
restaurant.

"This one looks nice," Matina said, pointing to a restaurant
where the rustic decor was visible from the street. Through large,
glass windows I could see a dark-beamed ceiling and a stone fireplace and an enormous wooden bowl piled high with fresh fruit on
a table in the entrance. We were shown to a table in an uncrowded
alcove in the rear of the dining room. The waiter hovered near us
offering suggestions and admiring us. It pleased him, I think, or
amused him, that we were mother and daughter. He had blazing
blue eyes that made love to you in one glance. Under his constant
gaze it wasn't easy to eat my tortellini in cream sauce. My mind
kept wandering. I imagined that the tortellini were slippery, tender
little kisses. Matina was relatively quiet, concentrating on her food.

The long, slow meal revived Matina, although of course she
couldn't let it end without groaning about having eaten too much.
Afterward, we went to the ladies' room and for a few seconds I
leaned against the maroon ceramic tile wall and watched my
daughter give her hair a few punishing licks with a mean-looking
wire hairbrush. Her hair looked wonderful—like ribbons of flame
that she was fanning to life. Silently I blessed that mop of hair and
resisted touching it, although actually I would have loved the
chance to brush it. "Ma, you know you're staring at me?" I lifted

my shoulders, didn't know what to say. I *was* staring at her. At that moment she had a certain radiance that captivated me.

By the time we paid the bill and shook hands with our waiter and went out into the narrow street, the afternoon had grown cloudy. Our map of the city showed that we were within striking distance of the Boboli Gardens. Matina wanted to find a bench with a panoramic view and not budge for the rest of the afternoon. As soon as we settled on the perfect bench, she began to tell me about her vacation in Wellfleet with her father and Marianne. "How was it?" I inquired mechanically. "I feel sorry for Dad," she said, trying to pique my interest. "Marianne wants to have a baby and Dad doesn't."

"How do you know he doesn't?" I had a strong feeling that Phillip would love a baby.

"Mother, *I* can tell. I'm going to be a good diagnostician. I pick up on small cues. I'm going to be like one of those Chinese doctors who can tell everything about a patient by looking into their eyes and at the tones of their skin and by tasting their urine. Dad's eyes looked strained; they looked dull."

"Maybe you're right, Matina," I said, backing off.

She yawned. "I'm exhausted," she said softly. "Let's go back to the Riccelli's. I have some kind of virus that keeps reappearing."

I suggested that we stay in Florence an extra day so that she could rest, but she insisted that all she needed was a short nap. I was tired, too. Matina and I were getting along well but still, she can exhaust me. My sense of her flip-flops from seeing her as fragile as a fawn—to seeing her as tough and gruff as a shaggy old bear. The strange part is that when she's the fawn, it's *my* power, *my* strength that she needs protection from. And then somewhere along the line being with her turns me into the fawn, and my life and my experience seems lightweight and thin and insubstantial. Most of the time I'm used to the flip-flopping; but sometimes it wears me out.

Matina slept from five-thirty in the afternoon right through to seven-thirty the next morning when she awoke rested and cheerful. In spite of the Riccellis' graciousness, we were glad to pack our bags, settle our bill, and take off. The place had an undeniable air of nostalgia that I was beginning to find stifling; it was something that in my line of work I have to guard against. I have to guard against romanticizing the preindustrial past. Everyone who works in the environmental field has to believe in nature's dedication to renewing itself. We have to believe in the future.

I drove while Matina, exhilarated after sleeping for fourteen hours, told me how wonderful her life was—how there'd been this brilliant, zany, sexy guy in her histology class whom she wanted to get to know, how great it was to be in one of the best medical schools in the world, how she couldn't wait till she got her hands on some real honest-to-goodness *living* patients with serious and subtle diseases, which she could diagnose with her own special finesse; and how lucky she was to have me as her mother.

"Really! Why?" I was initially flattered, then uncomfortable. "I'm no different from other mothers," I insisted. She was wearing my new lavender-and-white flowered wraparound skirt, which she'd asked to borrow this morning as though she were doing *me* the favor, which I suppose in a way she was. She knew I was tired of seeing her in her old jeans.

"You're more of a friend than a lot of mothers," she said.

"I'm your mother," I replied almost involuntarily, the words springing out of a kind of tribal memory, of mothers and daughters before me.

Then in more somber tones she told me that this was in all likelihood the last vacation we'd have together for a good many years. Soon she'd be a full-fledged physician. Never again would she be able to take time away from her work. Her words reached out to me like an icy hand in a handshake.

"Ma, there's something I haven't told you."

"What?" I asked, more sharply than I intended.

"You didn't look at the upper part of my arm, near my shoulder?" She pulled up the short sleeve of her shirt and twisted her arm around. "Dad didn't notice it either."

Reluctantly I took my eyes off the road and checked her upper arm. I saw a greenish blue profile of a face lodged in a crescent moon; the man in the moon, a side view. If it hadn't been needled on there for life, it would have been cute. "Is that permanent?"

"I knew you'd be mad."

"I'm not mad. . . ." and I wasn't. In fact I felt some unaccountable shred of relief.

"But you don't like it."

"It's cute; I only wish you could wash it off in about a week or two or a month."

"I like it," she said, and then leaned her head against the side window and closed her eyes. "I'll never be wearing an evening gown or a fancy wedding dress so it really doesn't matter."

"But you'll be wearing your skin," I said, more annoyed than I wanted to be.

·   ·   ·

We found a small hotel in a walled city about five miles from the Autostrada, not far from Siena. Our plan was to set up headquarters and set forth each day to another town. The proprietor, a large-boned woman about my age, had a serious stutter and preferred, each morning, to pen in our route on our map with a red Magic Marker rather than to explain in words where we should go and how we should get there. Matina thought our map was beginning to look like a textbook illustration of the circulatory system. In our stripped-down little Fiat she curled her legs up under her and grew peaceful. The serenity of the countryside soothed us both.

In Arezzo a day or two later, on a drizzly morning at the Church of San Francesco, I discovered the frescoes of Piero della Francesca, and was so captivated by their purity of line, the eloquence of gesture, the beauty of faces, that when a young French couple told me about a chapel in a cemetery in Monterchi about fifteen miles away that had another Piero fresco, I had to go. Matina, in a dreamy state, was willing though not eager. "Piero was an expert in Euclidean geometry," she murmured, one of those bits of information that kept popping out of her memory, "and he lived into his seventies but turned blind. What a cruel fate for a painter!" she exclaimed. "Probably only cataracts," she diagnosed a few moments later.

We entered the tiny, damp-smelling chapel, Matina somewhat less enthusiastically than I. She now liked driving in the car better than getting places. The fresco, painted onto one arched wall of the chapel, showed a stage with parted curtains, each held by down-to-earth female figures who one wouldn't suspect were angels except for their serviceable wings and unobtrusive halos. On center stage was the Virgin, a womanly figure in a full floor-length blue robe, one hand on her hip, the other resting lightly on the front of her dress which was straining open over the stomach and midriff. "Isn't she lovely!" I exclaimed. Matina agreed per-functorily, but complained of the chapel's clamminess. She'd wait for me outside. I lingered, staring at the fresco.

Here was the Madonna and she was tall and broad and had a strong neck and a doleful, introspective expression on her lovely face. Here was the Madonna with her dress bursting open in front, her hand on her stomach. Her hand *pointing* to her stomach. Here was the Madonna large with child: a solemn, rounded figure with a message for me. I experienced a shock of news: Matina was pregnant! Yes, I received that information as fully and precisely as the Virgin received the news of her conception from the archangel Gabriel. Matina was pregnant. My daughter the doctor-to-be with her own stethoscope and reflex hammer seemed to have no idea what her body was telling her; either that, or she wasn't going to tell me. And as soon as I realized that, my mind tried to find ways to bend the self-evident facts. She had simply put on a few extra pounds from the stress of her first year in medical school, and her fatigue and moodiness were a result of a minor virus she'd picked up during her fast-paced week of shows in Milan.

The sun had come out full force while I was in the chapel, and I found Matina basking in it, cross-legged, her eyes closed, on top of the hood of the Fiat. She looked chubby. I gauged that she had put on about twelve or fourteen pounds since I'd seen her last in June. I had a feeling that she was more than two months along, maybe even past the third month. No longer lithe; slightly awk-ward, my poor baby. I felt so sorry for her unluckiness. She was happy with her life the way it was, enthralled with medicine, ready to dive into its sea of claims.

Matina opened her eyes. "Ma, I keep taking these little naps." She seemed amused with herself, almost kittenish.

"Do you think you have something?" I asked, hoping she'd tell me that she had a virus or a sinus condition or was getting her period.

"Like what?"

Like a baby, I wanted to shout. "I don't know." I was on the verge of asking when she had had her last period, but something told me this wasn't the time or the place.

Matina kept her legs folded underneath her and stayed awake all the way back to our hotel. "Ma, it's been a nice day—but tomorrow let's go to Siena and go shopping." "Fine," I said. I would have preferred to fly back to New Jersey and get her to take a pregnancy test.

That night Matina appeared in her pajamas. "Remember when I used to like to comb and brush your hair?" I nodded. She'd been around seven or eight, and she liked to invent new hairdos for me. She'd part my hair in the middle and pull it back severely, or even braid it. She pretended she was a fancy hairstylist; her hands on my head had felt like a blessing. "Can I brush your hair now?" she asked. "Be my guest," I replied. She brushed my hair and I was sure that this was the moment when she was going to tell me about the baby, but she didn't breathe a word.

I fell asleep easily and woke with a start two hours later. The room was so dark and silent that I believed Matina was gone. I tiptoed the few steps to her bed and found her there, asleep on her side, a mountain range of girl. Reassured, I headed for the bathroom, sat in the dark, and let the tears come. I saw a baby—the perfect combination of Matina and Adam—curly-haired with velvety eyes and an expandable mouth that could take in the world; a honey drop, a pink blossom, a fuzzy ripe peach, a chickadee. My love for that baby knew no bounds, no bounds, and didn't diminish as the night pulsed along. I returned to bed but couldn't sleep.

I vowed to myself many times during the night that I wouldn't assault Matina with what I knew. I wanted to be gentle. I felt loving and tender and sympathetic. I wanted to say, I respect your needs and your decisions, I know you didn't choose this. I wanted to say, *You have the right to do what's right for you.* I wanted to say all the right things.

She hurried me along, claiming that she noticed she usually felt better after breakfast.

"You do?" I watched her wriggle into her jeans with the safety pin. "What do you make of that?"

"What *should* I make of it?"

She looked at me pityingly, sorry for my stupidity. I was trying to arrange a silk scarf around the neckline of my cotton sweater but was getting nowhere. I wasn't good with scarves, couldn't make them stay in the stylish loops and folds I intended. I asked Matina when she had had her last period. My tone was regrettably impatient.

"I'm not pregnant," she said angrily. I decided to believe her, and for a moment I felt happy, until she added, ". . . and if I am it's no big deal."

And I wanted to agree—it was no big deal.

The next day en route back to Milan, we stopped in Siena to go to a particular dress shop Matina knew about, but she ended up buying nothing. A while later on the Autostrada, she asked me if I'd stop the car so that she could get out and get in the back; she wanted to take a nap. I pulled over onto the shoulder of the road and she got in the back, and I started to drive again. I felt like the chauffeur, ignored, used. My mood turned sour. Matina took up so much space, she was so self-centered, so self-important and arrogant. She made me feel stupid and unimportant and stodgy and

fretful; full of warnings and doom and grief and misgivings and sti-
fled accusations. There were moments when I couldn't bear how
childish and shallow she was, how self-indulgent and silly.

And when I stopped being angry at her and myself, I thought
about the baby. My eyes teared, my throat ached. The baby was
taking on a definite personality. It was a baby who was curious and
easily amused. The baby was especially responsive to me, its grandmother. It gazed into my eyes with joyful recognition. In my imagination I was stocking up on basic toys—a play telephone, a
pull-along doggie on wheels . . . I was holding the toddler's hand at
the zoo . . . I was explaining the interdependence of all living
things—ecosystems, the importance of wetlands . . .

I couldn't believe where my mind was taking me. There
wasn't going to be a baby. It was no big deal. I found myself mut-
tering, I shouldn't know about this, I shouldn't know about this.
This wasn't my baby. That was the most pertinent truth: It wasn't
my baby. Moreover, it wasn't a baby; it was a tiny curled minute
shrimplike thing. In the light of reason, I could understand
Matina's not wanting to be a mother right now; and I believed that
a woman's freedom is hollow unless she can choose to have a baby
or not.

Suddenly Matina woke up. She was feeling nauseated, she
announced, as though it were my fault. My patience reached its
breaking point. I asked her whether she knew what the early signs
of pregnancy were. Obstetrics wasn't part of the curriculum until
the third year, she informed me, but Dr. Lang had mentioned
pregnancy in Anatomy class when he discussed the human pelvis.
"I don't mean the complex medical or physiological process of
pregnancy," I clarified, "but simply the ordinary everyday little
symptoms." I began to enumerate them. She was staring far out

across a field at a slow-moving tractor and murmured that she never wanted to have a baby, but I was still plodding ahead on my own educational trajectory: "It's possible to feel particularly emotional, you have to pee a lot . . ."

We soon entered the hazy environs of Milan, and my daughter asked me not to tell her father about her condition, her possible condition. I promised and didn't ask why. I thought of reaching for her hand but knew that that impulse was misguided. In the hotel room, which contained the same smoggy air as outside, Matina peed and then made a phone call. Speaking a mixture of English and Italian—I hadn't realized she could manage so much Italian— she made arrangements with a friend to spend the night. I couldn't tell whether it was a male or female friend and she declined to say. All she said was that it would be better for us both if she spent the rest of the time in Milan with people her own age. I agreed. Then instead of leaving right away, she sat down on her bed and emptied the contents of her khaki shoulder bag. I thought I glimpsed the plastic compactlike container of a diaphragm, but perhaps I was imagining things. Still, the idea of its uselessness made me sad. In a few minutes she bolted up and put on eye makeup. As she coated her eyelashes with mascara, she said, "Well, what do *you* think I should do?" My mind went blank, my mouth dry. *Have an abortion,* I wanted to say, but couldn't. "I don't know," I whispered, and she shot me a victorious look. I was sitting on the edge of the bed now and she was standing nearby looking down at me. She swept to the door, holding herself tall and aloof, her model's walk I assumed. Her parting words were that she'd meet me at the airport tomorrow an hour before flight time. "Fine," I said, and a raspy voice inside of me, a voice only I could hear, screamed, *I love the baby more than I love you, Matina.*

•   •   •

The plane's departure time was 12:20 and at 11:45 Matina hadn't yet shown up. At the last possible moment I underwent the security check, my suitcase X-rayed by some technicolor procedure that color coded its contents and transformed it into a weird rectangular animal with strange, yet all-too-familiar body parts—a couple of hangers, a cluster of jewelry, a belt buckle, a row of buttons like vertebrae. I received my seat assignment at the desk near the gate, and checked the clock every two and three minutes. No Matina.

Takeoff was delayed for thirty minutes and although the plane was by now hermetically sealed and disconnected from the terminal, I still expected Matina to appear. I sat in my seat imagining all the things I could have said to Matina: from offering to raise the baby myself—millions of grandmothers had done that— to giving her money for the abortion. And no possibility felt right.

The plane took off. I was in the air alone. The plane reached its cruising altitude. Outside, air; below, water, wrinkled water far below. In this middle zone between heaven and sea, my mind took a strange turn. I saw Matina clear as day in a pair of old jeans and a T-shirt, her hair wild as fire, and I saw the baby, downy as a peach. And then Matina's years and size began melting away, and slowly Matina became that tiny baby. I wanted to cradle her in my arms. I wanted to feel her body's heat. I whispered her name over and over again, but there was no sign that she heard me.

At the "Changing Careers" Conference

I always study those before-and-after pictures of people who've lost tons of weight and emerge lithe and lovely from their own body fat; or women with flippy new hairdos and makeovers, their old clothes updated by the simple addition of one bright scarf or a colorful belt or a change of buttons. Transformations, that's what interests me: how one thing turns into something else. That's why when my alma mater, Glassboro State, a medium-sized college in New Jersey, invited me to be on a panel of successful alumni in a conference called "Changing Directions — New Careers Along the Way," I accepted without hesitation. Panel members were promised private rooms in a brand-new dormitory, healthy meals, use of the gym, an evening of jazz, and a free sample of an expensive unisex cologne called Roma #4.

On a rainy morning in mid-May I packed my bag for the conference. When I was married to Phillip, packing was a mean chore, the closet jammed with clothes that Phillip liked and clothes that I liked. Phillip's taste leaned toward floral designs, stripes in strong colors, things with intricate borders, and fringes. His family had manufactured wallpaper since 1911, and patterns and designs were in his blood. I preferred solid colors, simple designs, collarless necklines, a plain white linen dress in summer. For the past couple of years I've bought only black and white. For that necessary splash of color I buy accessories, cheap punky things like a scarlet cowboy belt with studs and long loops of colored beads.

The letter that Glassboro State used to lure me here for this misbegotten gathering of people who can't stay on track was pretty much a lie. I never saw one bottle of unisex cologne, and there were no single rooms in the new dormitory, a ten-story tower that radically changed the pastoral character of the old campus. The man in charge of room assignments denied the promise of single rooms in the original invitation. I showed him the letter. It was an error, he insisted. I was disappointed. I'd pictured a solitary room with a bed, a desk, a bureau, and chair. And into this bare room I'd sneak my about-to-be-met lover, a man who'd changed directions along the way. Let's say, a man who'd been a talented thoracic surgeon but who'd renounced medicine for yoga, and who'd practiced sexual abstinence for years and was now ready for great safe sex with a terrific woman.

My roommate was making her bed when I entered. She had earlength straight gray hair with a line of bangs on her forehead. She looked up and said, "I'm Rosemary Bourne, and I imagine if you're anything like me, you're not all that happy to be having a roommate." She tucked in the sheet and then the blanket rather sloppily, no hospital corners, no military wrinkle-free tautness. She was a curator of a science museum in New Mexico; a paleontologist, an expert on fossils and bones. "I'm afraid I snore," she confessed.

What criteria of compatibility did the administrators of this conference use, I wondered, so that Rosemary and I ended up sharing a room? I introduced myself, Harriet Stedman, a nursery school education major when I was in college, and now a bureaucrat in New Jersey's Department of Environmental Protection. "I probably snore, too," I said, but my heart sank. Sleeping in a room with a stranger seemed like unbearable intimacy.

Lest I mistook Rosemary's gray hair for a sign that she was older than I, she was quick to inform me that she wasn't. "By the time I was thirty-three my hair was gray." She glanced at my chestnut-tinted hair. "I admire gray hair on other people," I confessed. "I admire *the principle* of gray hair." She chuckled and a bit of reserve crumbled. Her suitcase was open on top of her bed, and she removed a good-sized unopened package and leaned it up against the side of her dresser. I took out photographs of my children, Matina and Eric, and set them on my bureau.

Everything about Rosemary was minimal. One book, two outfits. "I've never been married," she announced after some time; "never had a live-in partner. Never had children. Never wanted them."

Did you ever want anything? I considered asking. I had grown wary of people who believed that the absence of desire was a sublime attribute. Phillip's mother had been that way: never stated a preference, a wish, a longing. Life was lived, it seemed, so that she could never be accused of being selfish. On the other hand, I never saw her act generously.

"I'm not good with children; I don't tend to find them amusing," Rosemary said, glancing at the photographs of my children, "and that's why I never wanted them." I smiled. It was perfectly fine with me if she hated children. I respect people who don't like children and don't have them. But when Rosemary stood at the closet with her back toward me, I gathered up Eric's and Matina's photographs and slipped them back into my suitcase.

"Never wanted children," Rosemary mumbled. "Never envied people who had them. There's something about not having children that's absolute freedom. Never thought my genes were so fantastic, anyway."

A shudder streaked up my back. I wanted my children; and sometimes I wanted my freedom. I tried not to be shy about my desires. I had what a very dear friend of mine called "a hard case of greed." I'd argued that it wasn't greed, it was *appetite*.

At six o' clock there was cocktail hour and then dinner for the two hundred panelists and alumni. Rosemary was sitting on the edge of her bed. "I'll rest a bit," she told me; "you go ahead." "Are you feeling okay?" "Absolutely fine," she said, folding her hands quietly on her lap. She looked like a prisoner who was preparing herself for execution.

The cocktail party was in the student center commons, halfway across the campus. I entered alone into the windowless room with a great expanse of shiny vinyl floor. We wore sticky name tags with our class year, and I compared people's appearances with their ages and knew that I was the object of the same kind of scrutiny. We were all citizens of the same country — Time; its heroes or heroines, its innocent victims. Rosemary Bourne never appeared.

At the dinner table I sat next to a lovely looking woman, Paula Palladino, whose competence and self-doubt were locked in a losing battle. I passed her the basket of rolls, the mashed potatoes, the butter, the salt. Whatever *I* said took on undue substantiality. I had written articles and pamphlets, I had children, colleagues, even an ex-husband — which suddenly seemed more intriguing to her than a plain ongoing husband. And whatever *she* said had to do with evanescent possibility: she was thinking about becoming . . . she was going to take a course in . . . she was going to put together a book about . . . . She had come to the conference to begin to network, she explained. She took my phone number and promised to invite me for dinner at her apartment in Manhattan.

The conference was sponsored by the Glassboro Alumni Association and the Office of Career Services for the benefit of alumni and undergraduates, and in the auditorium after dinner, Mrs. Louise McCarthy, the head of Career Services, addressed the group. She was a woman in a violet-colored tweed suit with those little granny half-glasses that you're not supposed to have to take on and off, but she did anyway.

We were here, she explained, to think about our work lives in a very new way—as flexible, as evolving, as organic—instead of in rigid categories, once-in-a-lifetime decisions. It would have taken me so many words to summarize what Louise McCarthy said about work in a sentence or two. I couldn't have stayed with "our work lives"; I would have spilled over into our personal lives—spiritual, material, love, sex, children, parents, history, and the environment, the planet—to name just a few of my areas of interest. I would have jumped in up to my eyeballs.

Louise McCarthy's voice was as smooth as a new highway. "There are two different approaches that people take in making important career changes: those who change directions little by little so that the small changes, the increments, are hardly noticeable; for instance, the phys ed teacher who over the course of fifteen years ends up owning and running a health club; and the person who takes a radical change of direction like our own graduate, Rick Novak, who's now on our music faculty, but who'd been a successful criminal lawyer and then turned to jazz, and who along with his combo will entertain us later this evening."

Mrs. McCarthy ended her talk with some statistics about Glassboro graduates and then introduced Rick Novak's band.

I listened to the jazz combo and stared at Rick Novak. He was short, animated, ecstatic, and younger than I was. Whatever he and that piano were doing, they were doing it together.

Afterward, I walked across the campus listening for the sound of peepers. None. None left in the state of New Jersey. But the night air was surprisingly sweet and the dampness wrapped around me like the lover I would have liked. I found my room on the sixth floor of the tower. Rosemary was sleeping, snoring lightly. I undressed in the dark.

In the morning I knew I had dreamed. A dream about bones, the bones of animals—the whole skeletons of animals, the great cathedral of curved ribs, the heavy femurs, skulls with elongated jaws bleached by the sun. "Close to the bone," that expression occurred to me but in no particular context. There was nothing awful about those dream bones. Not the remains of lives, but something promising, something truthful. Snakelike chains of vertebrae, jewelry on the desert floor. Georgia O'Keeffe territory. Then I understood I was dreaming Rosemary Bourne's dreams. And that was exactly why I didn't want to share a room with anyone. I was forty-six years old. I wanted my own dreams.

"I noticed you had put out some photographs of your children," Rosemary said as we were getting dressed for the day, "and then you slipped them back into your suitcase. I hope you didn't think I would object to looking at your children. May I see them?" I showed her the pictures and she studied them for a long time. "They look civilized," she finally said.

"What were you before you were a paleontologist?" I asked Rosemary during breakfast, assuming that she like most everyone else had changed careers. We were in the dining commons packing it away—oversized slabs of French toast doused in syrup, three sausages glistening with poisonous fat to which Rosemary had also succumbed. Fresh platters of French toast were placed before us.

"A music teacher," Rosemary replied, and I was determined not to ask her another question. I wasn't going to pump her for information. I was trying to learn restraint, a new kind of dignity that comes from holding back. I was trying to learn it at the same time as I was trying to teach it to my daughter, Matina, who was finishing her first year of medical school. "Matina," I would occasionally say, "rein in your feelings and your ideas and your questions. Contain them. Don't spill everything, don't express everything." "Oh mother . . ." she whined, "why the hell not?"

"Rosemary," I said suddenly, "I had a strange dream last night." My dream didn't interest her. She pierced her last piece of sausage on her fork and dragged it through the syrup and popped it into her mouth. Her eyes shifted away, into the dreamy distance.

There were three Ping-Pong tables in a large recreation room near the cafeteria, and after my third cup of coffee I challenged Rosemary to a game. I hadn't played in fifteen years. She had never played in her life. She was awkward at first, swiveling only from above the waist. We volleyed for a while. The feel of the game came back to me. I gave Rosemary some pointers. She had good instincts and beat me 21 to 11.

At ten the conference moved across the campus to Conway Hall, the main science building, and the panelists gathered on the stage of a lecture hall. Three men and five women. Rosemary Bourne was not among us. She was a resource person in the afternoon session, not a morning panelist. The only familiar face was Rick Novak, who had played piano in the jazz band the previous evening. He was a small, agile man who moved with grace and had an air of competent friendliness.

Four panelists preceded me. They spoke reasonably, using the buzzwords that had emerged from Mrs. McCarthy's guidelines, which she had sent to us about three weeks before. *Strategy objective, reassessment of goals, priorities, retooling, mentoring, networking, networking, networking* . . .

The panelists' talks were witty and informative; however, with each subsequent speaker, the number of buzzwords decreased. The exact steps of the changes, the actual "retooling process," as Mrs. McCarthy would have said, grew obscure. There was less and less mention of "strategy," and none of "networking." A couple of panelists had fallen in love with change itself. I glanced at Mrs. McCarthy. She wasn't entirely pleased. I think one career change was all she had in mind, thank you. We were supposed to be planful career strategists, not flaky misfits.

From that point on there was a sea change among the panelists. Rick slipped his prepared speech into his program folder and ad-libbed. "Years ago I heard Charlie Mingus talk about the great Charlie Parker and his genius for making music. 'You start by loving something,' Bird had said; 'that's where you start.'" He quoted Bird, his eyes dancing gleefully and softening with reverence. Then his mood changed. Instead of making the transition from lawyer to jazz musician and teacher sound like a well-reasoned assault on success, he spoke of "crawling around for a couple of years confused and lost in dark grottoes." And somewhere along the way, his wife left him and he had to declare bankruptcy. I glanced at Mrs. McCarthy; dark, slimy grottoes were not on her list of recommended strategies. I saw her mouth tighten and twist in disapproval even while she nodded encouragingly.

By the time it was my turn to speak, people had already exhausted the major points and I had to scramble for an organizing principle. I spoke about how finding what you love to do may be slow in taking hold and that life itself bears down with its own unpredictable necessities. Although I was trained as a nursery school teacher and worked in that field for years, I became intrigued with the lives of American women reformers. I wanted to write the biography of an incredibly bold, undiscovered American woman reformer. "But then Real Life happened," I explained. "My marriage died and my apartment building went condo and my daughter was about to start college, and I realized that my interest in resourceful American women was based on having to become one, not study them. That's when my cousin suggested I try for an entry-level position in the New Jersey Department of Environmental Protection. I'd have to move to New Jersey but I was willing to do that. Now I work in 'Solid Waste Management'—garbage: educating the public about where to put it, what to do with it once you get it there, and how to transform it." I could have gone on for a long time about my dream of being part of the effort to transform garbage into clean, safe energy, but I stopped myself—not easy for me, because I truly believe that clean, safe energy is the key to the future of the earth as we know it.

I made it my business to sit next to Rick during lunch. He was drumming his fingers on the table, some bumpy, syncopated beat I'd never be able to follow but that seemed to put a rapt expression on his face. When he saw me he remembered my name and even what I'd said. We talked about choice versus chance during lunch, which was indeed healthy—fish of the white, flaky kind—served by students who looked as though they'd never had a choice in their lives. "Do you have children?" he asked after the student waiter had cleared our plates and set down our desserts.

"A daughter, twenty-two, and a son who's seventeen." I anticipated shock when I told him my children's ages, but I detected none.

"My kids are young. Three and five-and-a-half. I've let them down," and he explained about his divorce last year.

I was quiet. Divorce, when it involves children, is a painful subject. It was hard to be wise and reassuring. The dining commons was practically empty. In other countries it was siesta time. Here the student workers were slathering the empty tables with watery suds. "Wait a minute," Rick said. "How about some fresh air?"

Guiding me outside, he showed me the new art and music area of the campus. "This is the art building." He pointed to a gray concrete structure that could easily have been mistaken for a parking garage. "Big studios with northern light." He tilted his chin toward the sky and May sunshine settled on his face.

We made our way around the edge of a faculty parking lot toward the south end of the campus. Every so often he glanced at me, sidelong looks. He noticed my dangling earrings, tiny blue giraffes, and touched one. "Funny earrings," he murmured, but I could tell his own children were still on his mind. He wanted to know how my children had fared. They had survived, I said; we had survived, their father had survived—in fact he was remarried to a young woman, happily. I was going to stop there, with a neatly-wrapped package, but I wanted to tell the truth: Matina and Eric lived with a yoke of loss, both yearning for a time when the family was as golden and perfect as a wedding ring.

I could feel a thick syrup of pain pass between us.

At the farthest side of the campus stood the renovated music building. I followed Rick upstairs to his studio. It was spacious with an expanse of newly sanded hardwood floor and three large windows that faced the edge of the campus, a marshy expanse. He showed me his piano, his recording equipment, a complicated sound system that had as many dials and buttons as a jumbo jet's cockpit. But when I had taken in all the high tech and hit a few keys of the grand piano, I wondered what I was doing there. Rick opened a closet and pulled out a futon, which he indicated I could sit on. He began to play "Sophisticated Lady" on the piano, and soon I was lost in sweet sound. A man's loving attention to his art is an aphrodisiac for most women. Would a man get turned on looking at a woman's etchings, listening to her read a poem or play the viola or talk about garbage?

Rick stopped playing and strolled over to his tape deck and put a tape on. It was the same piece, "Sophisticated Lady," his own rendition, I assumed. He fast-forwarded to the part at which he had stopped playing. The music rolled on and he motioned me to dance with him. We danced, at first awkwardly, then the song melted my gawkiness.

We danced for a long time, separate and up close. He was listening and moving; his body was reading the sound. Our moves began to ricochet off each other like good conversation. His eyes were as dark as coffee beans. He was younger than I was, and shorter. Say about six or eight years or more and four or five inches. His life was in a state of semicontrolled turmoil. I was totally drawn to him. Dancing triggers some biochemical change in my brain. We started kissing and we kissed until we were sure we wanted each other badly, and then we stoppped. We had to. I mean, I was a "resource person" in the afternoon program of the conference. I had assumed professional obligations and I wouldn't shirk them.

Rick pressured me to play hooky. "We can go to Atlantic City or to the shore, or to Philadelphia, or you could come to my apartment." The way he put together an agenda thrilled me. There were times when I wanted to be rescued from myself. That's the hardest part of living alone: drowning in your own sea of self; then having to mastermind your own rescue.

"What if I meet you around five or five-thirty," I offered. "I'll drive over. Give me directions. I can't skip out on the afternoon session." I had volunteered to be a resource person in the afternoon because so many young people were clamoring for careers in the environmental field. It's the unexpected opportunities for educating people that I love about my work: speaking in front of town planning committees or high school students or even the state legislature.

Rick sharpened a pencil and, kneeling on the floor, drew a map. He traced over the pencil-drawn route with a red pen, showing me my route with tiny arrows.

"We can go out for dinner," I said.

"Don't worry. I'll take care of it," Rick assured me. "I know how to cook. In fact I've developed a recipe with shrimp and rice and peppers that I named after Thelonius Monk."

A short while later, in the dining commons, I sat alone at one side of a long table with a cardboard sign in front of me that read "Careers in Environmental Protection" and listened in ten- or fifteen-minute intervals to young people's anxieties about the endangered planet. Soon I had to shake loose from their paralysis of doom. I tried to help them translate their concerns into specific careers and jobs. I tried to sell a couple of bright-eyed students on a future in solid waste management. Garbage? they said with dismay, and I nodded.

"Welcome," Rick murmured almost apologetically.

"Hi. No problem getting here. Your map was great."

His eyes seemed to take me in in sweeping glances that moved around and behind me but avoided my eyes. He was painting me in watercolors, dissolving me. I looked past him. The living room was bright with a touch of Mexico, and one wall had a bookcase. In a certain way a person's books spell out his life. I checked Rick's books, the ones that he had only recently worked so hard to separate from his wife's, and imagined them intermingled with mine. The romance of the perfect union: my books were full of sweetness and light, about infants and early childhood and strong, good women. His were about criminals and the criminal mind, repeat offenders, death sentences, marginality, voices from prison. On the bottom shelf, lying flat, were children's books. I kneeled to see whether he had any of Eric's and Matina's favorite picture books. He crouched behind me and nuzzled my ear. I turned my face toward his lips and our lips touched, and mine were eager, but Rick drew back. "Let me show you the rest of the place," he offered, and I was pained by the brush-off.

His small bedroom was part of the tour. I stood in the doorway cautiously, with nothing to say, as though I were looking at an apartment I might be interested in renting. He pointed out that the room had cross-ventilation, a corner room—small but airy. The bed wasn't made and whatever had gone on in it certainly excluded me. "Excuse my unmade bed," he mumbled.

Finally he led me to the kitchen with its dining alcove and I could see the table set for four. I saw a bottle of wine on the counter and hamburger patties neatly laid out on tinfoil. So much for "shrimp Thelonius," I thought. "Who else is coming?" I asked, and Rick said, "Samantha and Thomas." At first I thought they were friends of his, then I remembered that those were his children's names. It had honestly slipped his mind that his kids were coming to stay for the rest of the weekend. "I can't believe I came that close to forgetting," he confided.

My disappointment over not being alone with Rick deepened into sorrow. I tried to hide it. Sorrow was unreasonable, extreme. I covered by telling him how when Phillip and I first separated we had a hard time with schedules, and poor Eric became so jittery about time that he developed a habit—almost like a tic—of constantly checking his watch. I bought him a Walkman and gave him money for tapes thinking that music might soothe him."

"Did it?"

"I don't think so."

"It was a good idea, anyway," he said, and I could tell that he liked me for thinking that music, any music, had healing powers.

I glanced at my watch, wondering what time his children were arriving—a three-year-old and a five-year-old, the ages I knew best. Children were the essence of themselves at that age and yet still close to a mysteriously magical world. I loved their eyes, how they focused inward and out at the same time. I could almost feel Samantha's and Thomas's amperage beaming into the apartment ahead of them, buzzing and whirring like a billion insects on a summer night. But soon the scene at the dinner table, if I stayed, began to play out on my mind's screen, an awful sitcom, the children's worries about the terrible changes in their lives and who I was translated into glasses of milk careening to the floor and attention-getting antics and chatter escalating to screeching tantrums. I could see little Thomas's face turning scarlet and snot running from his nose into his mouth and then the unstoppable heaving sobs.

I remembered in a rush that I liked my life the way it was. I didn't want to be rescued. I didn't think I'd ever want to marry again—even if God asked me.

"I can't stay," I said.

"Please stay," he urged; "they're good kids." He turned away from the stove and was holding a spoon in midair. "They're great kids. Thomas needs eye surgery," he said. I told him I was sure his kids were wonderful but there'd be hell to pay. His kids wanted him, not me. "Trust me on this one," I said, but I could see he couldn't.

"Just eat supper with us," he urged; "it's all ready. I have everything ready to go."

On the way to my car I passed a pretty blond woman holding the hands of two young children, a girl and a smaller boy. Rick's family, I realized. The little boy was wearing eyeglasses. It was the eyeglasses on that little guy that made my heart go out to him. I wanted to hold that little boy on my lap, I wanted him to lean back against my breasts. For a second I thought, *Yes, I could love that child.* My comfort and skill with young children tugged at me. Give in and eat the hamburger, drink the wine. As far as little kids were concerned, I had a bundle of tricks up my sleeve: stories, games, and a calmness borne of years of experience. But it was the father I wanted.

I expected Rosemary to be at the dining room when I returned, but she was sitting on the edge of her bed holding a heavy-looking white bone. I was glad to see her. Her watery eyes looked brighter. The bone was resting on her lap. I couldn't figure out whether the bone was a trophy, an object of scientific investigation, or a religious relic.

"This arrived by UPS just as I was leaving for the airport in Albuquerque, so I threw it into my suitcase," she explained. "It's amazing," she said; "it' wonderful." I nodded. "Yes, it's amazing," I agreed.

My interest in the bone didn't make Rosemary want to talk. All she would say—and that in a whisper—was that the bone was a femur and it was absolutely fascinating and important. "A femur of what?" I asked, wondering if it was man or beast's, ancient or recent. Beast, I hoped, but she declined to say. I remembered Matina talking about bones and hacksawing through the bones of cadavers, how challenging it had been to make a good, clean cut. It was strange to me, this kind of ease with body parts.

Silent and withdrawn, Rosemary now lolled in a trance, staring at the bone. The bone was white and dry. Lifeless. I imagined that she wanted to see that dry bone turn into a great leafy tree or a lilac bush in bloom or a lush ripe peach or a person she could love, someone who might say, *Here hold out your hand and take this, you'll never guess what it is.* Someone who might say, *C'mon, I'm taking you somewhere you've never been.* Rosemary desired more than she knew. Or was I talking about myself? I glanced at my watch. Not far from here hamburgers were being eased onto open hamburger buns; ketchup was jetting forth from a ketchup bottle; a man was pouring milk. I was thirsty.

Rosemary was willing to be coaxed into dinner, but it was the promise of a game of Ping-Pong that got her moving. The game was intense. Rosemary's serve was fast and accurate; she was suddenly great at slamming. "You're going to beat me," I said, and Rosemary's expression was so full of victory that I felt like laughing, and with that urge came a rolling wave of excitement. I didn't care who won. Possibility bounced back and forth in one long volley.

The Provider

P hillip, acting on impulse, strode out of his office a little after eleven A.M. The distance from the showroom of his whole-sale wallpaper firm on Third Avenue to his four-room apart-ment was only a couple of miles, and feet were the fastest means of getting there in the middle of a workday. Mild April weather. Pale sunlight on the spiky city. Traffic, even taxis, stopped compliantly at red lights; people peered at the sky and shifted their raincoats to their arms. Halfway home, Phillip ducked into a ready-to-go gour-met food shop and bakery and bought small quantities of imported cheeses, three-quarters of a pound of gingered chicken with wal-nuts, a half a pound of roasted veal with parsley pesto, and four sesame-seed rolls.

Marianne, his wife, was at home, sick. A twenty-four-hour virus or simply fatigue. Nothing more serious. He wasn't worried. In fact, her unexpected return from jogging, her complaints of "no zip" and a low-grade headache had actually pleased him. Not exactly pleased, but soothed, in some inexplicable way. And it wasn't because he believed she was pregnant. He knew for a fact that she wasn't: Her period had come and gone two weeks earlier.

"You're allowed to be sick once in a while, sweetie. Rest, take a nap," he'd suggested as though she had never been sick before. Indeed, once when they were talking about childhood ills, Marianne had told him that she'd never had measles or German measles or whooping cough or mumps, and only a light case of chicken pox. By the time she was born there'd been immunizations for most of those illnesses. He, on the other hand, was sure he had had them all, along with the little treats that went with them — comic books, airplane models, a new set of Crayola crayons, meals served to him in bed by his mother.

Marianne had stood in the middle of their bedroom, with its top-of-the-line bamboo-textured wallpaper, and refused his advice about staying in bed. She put on her shiny little running shorts and black tights, but when she came back twenty minutes sooner than usual, her face was as white as the porcelain vase on their dresser top. At that point she didn't know whether to go forward — shower and get dressed and go to work — or retreat. Going forward was important to her. Life was short, you had to get on with it. Decisions had to be made, plans put in gear, chores — and even pleasures — accomplished.

"I'll call the agency and tell them that you'll be out sick today," Phillip offered. Finally as a way of agreeing, Marianne stripped off her tights, her shorts, her sweatshirt; naked and wordless, she slithered her slim, sweet body into bed. He stroked her hair and let his hand follow the valley of her backbone down under the covers. "Hmm . . ." she murmured almost inaudibly, "maybe it's not so bad being sick."

On the phone with the secretary at the social service agency where Marianne worked, Phillip took the liberty of saying that Marianne might be out sick for a couple of days. The secretary sounded alarmed—Marianne had never missed a single day of work—and again he noted some small comfort in the possibility of her illness.

He put a glass of ice water on the bed table. A faint thank you spiraled up from the pale blue pillow. Her hand reached for his, tugging him toward her. He promised to leave work by mid-afternoon, and kissed the top of her head lightly and then touched his lips to her forehead, which seemed quite warm. By the time he left she was fast asleep.

Now, only a couple of hours later, Phillip let himself into the apartment quietly, although he expected, perhaps unreasonably, to find Marianne awake, waiting for him. She was sleeping exactly the way he had left her, a narrow column under the quilt on her side of the bed, her hand underneath her cheek, the skin of the exposed cheek pale and translucent, her eyebrows dark. Sick, she looked younger than her twenty-nine years. He believed that even though she was asleep, her lips were shaping invisible kisses that sailed upward and landed on his mouth.

The telephone on the bedside table had been unplugged; Marianne must have done that after he left.

Marianne was always wanting to unplug the phones. Before dinner. Then again in the evenings between nine and eleven for "some uninterrupted time together," and also on Sunday mornings and sometimes on Saturday evenings. "Time to disconnect," she would announce, moving around their apartment, clicking telephone cords out of wall sockets. She believed in protecting some time alone with him. He treasured their time together also, but it made him uneasy. As a father he couldn't cut himself off, couldn't not be immediately available for those nightmare emergencies that parents imagine, or for the ordinary events of their daily lives: after all, Eric was only seventeen and Matina twenty-two. Pretending not to be home seemed treacherous to him; however, to Marianne, younger than he, the telephone was simply another piece of electronic equipment, like the computer or the automatic time-controlled coffeemaker or the CD player or the VCR, not an inviolable link to the world.

He left the bedroom and tiptoed into the sunny living room, noting that the phone on the desk had also been unplugged. (So she *had* been up after he'd gone off to work.) Three tall windows faced south on a tiny, square park, landscaped with a few gingkos, a willow, and Norway maples, a fountain in the shape of an airborne seal with its nose poised skyward (in the summer a stream of water spouted from that nose), and benches rooted in concrete so that they couldn't be stolen. Phillip stood discretely at the side of the center window. He could see four or five bedraggled men with their bundles and carts. A man with a gray ponytail, a black man with a raggy, old coat—both old-time regulars. So far this spring he had not yet spotted the woman with the two dogs, the relatively neatly dressed older woman, who over the past few years had fascinated his son, Eric. "That's an L.L. Bean hat she's wearing, Dad." Or, "How can she afford dog food?" Or, "Doesn't her cart look like a Roman chariot and the dogs like horses?" Or, "I'm going to go up to her one of these days and ask her what her dogs' names are."

Eric and Matina and he had become intrigued with these people who lived in the park. Marianne tried to ignore them. She saw enough misery and homelessness on her job. And one day a couple of years ago Eric marched across the street, stood in front of the woman with the dogs, and asked her if he could pet them. She shook her head No without looking at him. "Dad, she just said 'no' in a mean voice, but I sat down next to her on the bench and I was quiet, and I noticed all these scars and scabs on her fingers and hands and I tried not to stare at them, and finally after a long while she said, okay, and I petted the dogs and asked her their names." Olaf and Bambi—those were their names, Phillip recalled.

Phillip watched the ponytailed man take a can of soda out of one of his plastic bags and pass it around to the others. In three seasons out of four, people lived in this tiny postage-stamp park. Phillip used to call them *bums*; then he progressed with the times and called them *the homeless*; and now he and a couple of neighbors secretly referred to them as *the gentry*, imbuing them with a certain nobility and distinction, and maybe denying for a time their poverty and need, their destitution. Strange how we coexist, Phillip thought, however unequally: they live and we live on a street where the most recently renovated condos in old brownstones sell for three-quarters of a million dollars. We have walls and ceilings, they don't. We have hot water and toilets and heat, they don't. They suffer and we don't. And yet, we share this street with an odd kind of goodwill.

In the middle of the night while the housed were sleeping in their clean comfortable beds, the gentry sorted through his garbage, finding the stale croissants, the clotted fettucine alfredos, the apples with soft brown spots, the rubbery carrots. The way he knew this was because he had heard the garbage can covers fall to the sidewalk one night at three A.M. The tinny clanking jolted him out of a restless sleep, and he went to the window and watched two men divvy up the cast-off junk of his life. His half-eaten food, his holey, half-worn socks, his boxer shorts with the rip in the crotch that neither he nor Marianne, with all good intentions, would ever get around to mending, the hair from their hairbrushes. What the gentry found in the light of the streetlight, they evaluated and carted off across the street to where, for a brief five or ten minutes during the dead of the night, they had trusted their precious plastic bags to remain unguarded.

Phillip, who had observed all this in the middle of the night while Marianne was sound asleep, watched them pack and unpack and repack their precious bundles. He rarely saw them eat, but he knew that they did, and knew that one or two of those men would, before this week was over, be eating bits of imported cheese or gingered chicken. Throwing away his garbage was no longer a private act.

More and more he'd come to feel responsible, like a good host, and he would put something wholesome and substantial in his trash—a wedge of Swiss cheese or a couple of peanut butter sand-wiches in baggies. Sometimes in the summer, when one or two of the men stripped off their shirts to shower in the spray of water that arced from the seal-fountain's nose, and lathered themselves with a bit of soap, and soaked and washed their raggedy hair, he felt a weird kind of pride, as though his people were doing okay.

He turned away from the window, wanting to reconnect the phones, knowing that Marianne would want them to stay unplugged. There were times when she didn't even want to know whether there were calls on the answering machine. Of course, who were the calls for? Usually for him. Matina mostly—his daughter, making sure that he remembered the past, the *real* fam-ily and the *real* life. Or Harriet, his ex, with some strategic question or tidbit of news. Or Eric being a good son. On occasion his business associate Rick called about an order that had been delayed or some other problem. Or it was his secretary with a message that couldn't wait. His mother, a widow, never called. "Sons call mothers; mothers don't call sons," she'd pronounced, a dictum she apparently lived by without knowing why.

Nonetheless, as soon as he heard Marianne stirring in the bedroom, he reconnected the phone and no sooner than he had, it rang and it *was* Matina. "How'd you know I was home?" His secretary had told her, she said. "What do you want, honey?" She rambled on about the news of the sudden death of a famous rock star after routine surgery still reverberating in the hospital with which her medical school was affiliated—"heads are going to roll," and about Eric's big performance at his school for dance in North Carolina in June. "Are you going, Dad?" "I don't know. Is Mom?" "Of course she is." "Well, then I probably won't." "That really sucks, Dad. Poor Eric, he gets the shit end of the stick."

Marianne was awake now, listening from under the covers, trying to be patient, he could see. One breast with its nipple like a curious little eye was peeking out from under the quilt. The telephone had a fifteen-foot cord and he could stroll back and forth past the bedroom door with it.

Partly for Marianne's benefit—to soothe her, to reassure her, he said, "Matina, Eric can take care of himself. If he really wants me to see him perform, he'll tell me. He's very good at making his needs clear."

"I don't think he is."

A voice from the bedroom whispered loudly, "Why do you keep getting embroiled in her ridiculous, irrational arguments?"

Embroiled was the key word.

Matina went on registering her concern for her brother. "Sometimes when he's at your place, Dad, he goes out to see a film he doesn't really want to see," Matina insisted, "so that you and Marianne can be alone. He told me that. He's so tuned in to *your* needs." "He goes because he wants to see the movie," Phillip argued. Tempted to launch into the reasons behind *her* excessive concern for Eric—her desire to make him feel guilty and connected—Phillip stopped himself. The expression on Marianne's face, which he could see from the living room, was one of serious disapproval. Not angry disapproval—but loving, worried, serious disapproval.

His way of making up to Marianne was by fixing them lunch and bringing it to her in bed. Her color returned, she seemed hungry. He sat alongside the bed on a curvy mauve Queen Ann–type chair that they had found in an antique shop in Wellfleet last summer and reupholstered on a rainy Saturday a month ago while the phones were disconnected. Fixing up the apartment was a great shared activity. They were learning to use small power tools, to do simple repairs and cabinetwork. Marianne was skillful and precise, excellent at measurements, a genius at fractions; moreover, her eyesight was perfect. A design for cherry bookshelves was pinned to the bulletin board in the kitchen. "I think we're almost ready to tackle it," Marianne had said the other day, after their success with three small shelves in the bathroom. The two of them were a good team. They had a list of new tools they planned on buying: a battery-operated screwdriver, a belt sander, and a router.

She ate her sesame-seeded French roll, a small piece of gingered chicken. They drank cold glasses of fortified skim milk. The milk was something new.

"Sweetheart, how come you came back from work so soon?" She gazed at him appreciatively.

Her question took him aback. Why *had* he rushed home so soon? Because there was a certain electric force coming from Marianne that had drawn him all the way home.

"I'm glad you did," she continued when she realized he was staring at her. She reached for his hand and held it, a gesture, he assumed, of forgiveness for backsliding into *embroilment* with his daughter Matina.

He was still trying to answer her question. "I just wanted to come home. I couldn't concentrate. I was worried that you had a fever."

"Phillip, I hate it when I badger you about Matina. I'm sorry."

He asked her if she wanted tea or coffee, a sliver of cheesecake or a cookie. She shook her head slowly. "I want you," she crooned, patting and smoothing a small circle of bed next to her. He carried the tray into the kitchen, then returned—to the chair. Her mouth turned down; she pouted playfully. Uncomfortable, Phillip reached down to pick up one of her shoes, which had gotten caught under the chair. The heel was rundown, the shoe scuffy and in need of polishing. He made a mental note to take the shoes to the repair shop on Ninth Avenue.

She commented on his distractedness, asked him again why he'd rushed home. Did she seem *that* sick this morning? It was more that he wanted to make sure she rested and slowed down, he tried to explain. Lately she'd been on a "kind of treadmill." "Treadmill?" The word made absolutely no sense to her. "Getting up early, making the bed, jogging, going to work, doing small projects in the evening, food shopping on Saturdays . . . " he clarified. "It's not a treadmill," Marianne said, "it's our life, I love it." She paused, searching his face for a couple of seconds. "Are you okay, sweetheart?"

"Of course," he smiled, noticing now that she had been eating her lunch and sitting up in bed with her breasts bare. He'd in fact been too distracted to take that in. Her nipples were the same color as the Queen Anne chair he was sitting on.

"Darling, it's nap time," she said, caressing the quilt again. He nodded but stood up; he had to refrigerate the perishable food he'd left on the kitchen counter. In the kitchen, out of Marianne's sight, rewrapping food, loading butter and cheese and veal into the refrigerator, he thought about having children—babies, human life—and all that went into their sustenance. His heart pounded, he bit his lip. Each child that was born was a journey. He turned on the cold water faucet and stood at the sink with the water running. A long journey. A journey *into*, not *away from*, the webbed and knotted, complicated center of things. He recalled in detail Matina's birth more than twenty-two years ago. A natural birth. He was in the delivery room, robed in sterile green—a doctor's coat, a cap, a mask—and Harriet with her thighs violently spread in horrible stirrups, her stomach a volcanic dome, and then waiting, waiting. And finally, the baby's head—crowning. That was the word! Crowning. Crowning and coronation. A sensation of golden light. "I can see the head," he announced. And then the pulsing and pushing forth and plowing forward of the glistening wet head—and then the waiting and struggle for the shoulders. He thought he was going to faint with the baby half-out and half-in, waiting for the rest of it to be born, but when he glanced at Harriet he saw that she knew what she had to do. And soon the shoulders and little chest appeared, pinpoints of nipples, and then the thick, spiraled veinous-blue cord, like a shining and slippery wet telephone cord, and the rest of the baby sliding out easily now, caught in the doctor's rubber-gloved hands.

Then later, after the statistics, and after the washing and

bundling, Harriet and he had unbundled her, inspecting her minute perfection, celebrating their clever craftsmanship. They were young and expected joyous outcomes. Matina—if she were a girl born in the morning; Eve—if she came in the evening; Aurora—if she arrived at dawn. It was 9:30 A.M. Matina was their little gypsy, they decided giddily, with her black hair and her ruddy complexion. Harriet, triumphant, was eating a gigantic bowl of chocolate ice cream—that's all she wanted for breakfast—and they chattered about their little gypsy, her sparkling perfection, her endearing personality, her bright future.

From coronation to embroilment, Phillip mused, and he felt sad for Marianne who he was sure must have fallen asleep by now, tired of waiting for him and wondering why so much water was rushing down the sink drain when there were so few dishes and no pots or pans to wash, and nothing, really, to wash; and he didn't feel sad for Matina because he knew the measure of Matina's strength.

The quilt covered Marianne completely; even her long hair was tucked under it. A patch of cheek turned away from him. He eased his body onto the bed, lying on top of the quilt, and as soon as he was settled Marianne opened her eyes and turned on her side, facing him. Was he angry at her? she wanted to know, and he of course said No, which was the truth. He loved her delicacy, her goodwill, her almost-Japanese self-containment, her considerateness. He loved the deliberate way she managed the small rituals of daily life: making strong fresh Hawaiian coffee from beans she ground herself, changing the linen on their bed at least twice a week. How impressed he'd been when she had figured out how to use their complicated cappuccino-maker. He liked baking French bread with her, then moving on to an Italian loaf with olives. Believe it or not, they had a good time at the laundromat.

"Well if you're not angry at me, Phil, please get under the covers. Please, just a tiny afternoon nap." Her hand fumbled with the buttons on his shirt.

He stood up and undressed slowly while she watched. He wasn't jumping at the opportunity. His reluctance pained her, he could see that.

How could he explain his idea, a silly idea, of not trying this month? Of deliberately not trying.

Marianne held up the top corner of the quilt. A puff of air heated by her body stirred the airspace as he slid under the covers. Her body was a fresh warm roll, his was cold toast. She set to work warming him, sweetly, with enthusiasm.

Not only had he thought about not trying, but the idea had occurred to him of using contraception, even condoms, like the rest of the world were being urged to use.

With her hand on his pelvis she turned him toward her, smoothed him up and down, petted and stroked him with her hand the way he had once begged her to do, as though he were the sleekest, most hot-blooded thoroughbred horse. Lightly she stroked him all over, but not the part that was most sensitive. No, she was taking her time. He eased onto his back. Take your time, he thought, and then he imagined calling out "Stop," like a policeman regulating traffic. Stop! Halt! Red light! Do not proceed! His eyes focused on a framed reproduction of a Georgia O'Keeffe painting on the wall across the room. Creamy white flowers, their deep innermost parts splayed open. The petals barbed at their tips with baroque curlicues which he had never noticed before.

Pressing herself against him, Marianne climbed on board, her narrow body not quite covering his, pinning his upper arms down with her hands with a strength that surprised him, kissing his eyelids and the delicate crescents underneath them, kissing his mouth, licking it, and slowly—ever so slowly licking a long line from his chest straight down into the warm hollow of his navel and past it. She took him in her mouth, and then when he was hard and explosive, she uncurled herself, moved upward again and settled the warm oven of herself down, down around him.

Afterward, Marianne dozed off. He listened to her sweet breath, saw the faint blue vein that lined its way down her jaw and slender neck. Disentangling from their embrace, he rose from the bed, stepped into his underwear and, barefooted, made his way to the living room. The afternoon sunlight was blurry now, and a sluggishness descended, even on the avenue traffic—trucks having made their deliveries, buses on the avenue bringing children home from school, everything moving slowly, heavily. Phillip stood again at the window watching the gentry. Ten or twelve men now congregated. A couple of them had a big rusted Dumpster on wheels in tow like a baby carriage, and they wheeled it around the park and out in the street, and from his vantage point on the third floor, Phillip could peer down into the filthy metal container. He could see a man wrapped in a black coat, curled up on his side on a bed of newspapers, taking his turn to sleep in this giant-sized baby carriage, or maybe he was sick. He could see the matted hair and a hand clutching a shiny, lumpy dark-brown garbage bag. What a sickening stench that baby must have! That forgotten baby beyond hope. Oh God, he thought, whose baby was that!

Phillip scanned the park benches for the lone woman, Eric's favorite, who for years had been a daytime regular—perhaps not a bona fide homeless. She had a faint aura of distinction, of gentility with her clean clothes and funny hat; possibly a room somewhere, a bed, a chair, a toothbrush. Phillip's eyes roved the park, and finally he spotted her. She wore a gray jacket and her L.L. Bean hat, and two long white braids stuck out from under the hat. She was back, she was back. It was April and she was back sitting on the bench next to the seal fountain, her dogs Olaf and Bambi resting in front of her. The dogs were tied to the shopping cart with thick rope, their heads up and alert, guarding her the way the two lions guard the entrance to the Forty-second Street Public Library, the way he tried to guard his family.

Chicken Livers

Matina was highlighting sentences about the disorders of pregnancy: ectopic pregnancy, toxemia, spontaneous abortion. The textbook made pregnancy sound like one vast opportunity for disease and misfortune. The more she studied, the more certain she was that obstetrics wasn't for her. She wanted to be part of a roving rescue team that would jump out of medically equipped vans, descend on people holing up in derelict buildings or abandoned subway stations, and administer on-the-spot emergency care. There was a man who lived in the small park across from her father's apartment who she was sure had Parkinson's disease. She'd approach him, open the neckline of his filthy shirt, and listen to his heart. "Now hold your breath," she'd say softly, moving her stethoscope around to his back. "Now cough." She imagined sitting on the bench next to him, under a Norway maple, scribbling a prescription for the most up-to-date medication.

Gently she dumped Carlos from her lap where he'd nestled asleep while she studied and went into the kitchen to fill his water bowl. She'd never in her life had a pet. Her father was too fastidious and her mother probably would have resisted spending hours in a veterinarian's waiting room.

Ever since their long-anticipated week's vacation together in Italy, she'd been hating her mother. They hadn't spoken since Matina walked out of their hotel room in Milan. Her mother had left two messages on her answering machine, but Matina had returned them only when she knew Harriet would be out. Perhaps *hate* was too strong a word; but *dislike* was too mild. Her mother's face was an open book, her disappointment or pain always too apparent. Sometimes her mother tried to hide her feelings but it rarely worked. In fact on their trip in Tuscany, her suffering had spilled over in any number of small but obvious ways: her sad eyes, her fitful sleep, her wistful references to Matina's ex-boyfriend, Adam. If only her mother were more focused on her own work and less on her children. After all, she had an important job working for the State of New Jersey in their division of solid waste management. She was one of those people responsible for shipping New Jersey's garbage to western Pennsylvania. Her mother's lack of focus bothered her, her nostalgia for the past—not her personal past, but some distant pastoral time when large families worked happily together on farms, when air quality wasn't an issue and garbage posed no threat.

Matina dialed Harriet's number in Weehawken. It was Saturday. The voice on the answering machine was gentle, almost syrupy, coaxing information from callers. The message that Matina left was measured. "This is your daughter. Just calling to say hello." And then, for the fun of it, she tried getting Carlos to meow into the phone.

For one despairing moment she hoped her mom would answer.

As a second-year medical student, her life was nothing but books and lectures and observing other people doing important things. She decided she needed a break from studying and her small living room needed a paint job: a fine diversion. Within a half hour she was swinging two buckets of paint up Second Avenue. Two walls bright tangerine, two walls white. Outdoors, a late afternoon wind from the river was cycloning scraps of trash and black soot around her. She swerved into Safeway and bought a pound of chicken livers.

The tangerine paint was scrumptious; it rolled on the wall like icing on a cake. She threw open windows. Her boom box was blaring an old David Byrne tape. She opened another beer. When the paint was dry, she'd hang up her poster-size illustration of the circulatory system. The blues and reds would be wild against the tangerine wall. Perhaps she'd find a comparable poster of the nervous system or maybe even the female reproductive system with its graceful symmetry, its hydralike fallopian tubes. Carlos slunk out of the bedroom and settled on top of her feet, shackling her to the spot. Carefully she slipped her feet out from under him.

She rolled on the white paint, but the roller was oozing tangerine, marbleizing the wall. She wished that her father and his young wife, Marianne, both so neat and fussy, could see the mess she was making.

In the midst of her whirlwind of redecoration, the buzzer rang. She spoke into the apartment house phone. "Who is it?" "Mom." Her mother's voice had a pleading urgency. Matina pressed the button and pictured her mother striding into the murky lobby. She knew she'd be wearing a black wool suit with some weird, funky accessories.

Matina waited to open the apartment door until she knew her

mother was leaning into it. Yes, she was wearing a black wool suit, but black was no longer a viable color for her; it washed out her complexion to gray; and the pin on her lapel wasn't funky; it was downright childish—a plastic Halloween pumpkin. Reflexively they hugged. She could feel her mother crumple ever so slightly against her. "Sit down, Ma."

Harriet pulled herself upright, remained standing.

There was a lot to ask, to say. There was nothing to say. Why was her mother here? Matina had vowed not to talk about what had happened in Milan after her mother had flown back home: fast work—in an elegant, high-tech, female gynecologist's office. The latest procedure, almost too quick. Uncomfortable but not unbearable. An atmosphere of stainless-steel tables, instruments, and no recriminations. If she hadn't told Adam, she wasn't going to go into details for her mother. Somewhere in the middle of Tuscany her mother had guessed she was pregnant, even before *she'd* realized it. Her mother was a shrewd diagnostician.

"I called first but you were out. I prayed you'd be back by the time I got here."

"I'm glad you came," Matina said. "Sit down, Ma," she repeated.

"Looks pretty, honey." Harriet scanned the walls, then scanned her, her eyes X-raying her stomach with maternal worry and general grievousness. She sank onto the couch, which was sitting under a sheet in the middle of the floor. "Be careful," Matina warned, "there may be splatters on there." Harriet didn't seem to mind. Matina offered yogurt, a beer, tea or coffee, but her mother had already eaten dinner. In fact, she felt a little queasy. She'd had an upsetting day.

"I called *you* today," Matina said. "Left a message on your machine."

"Strange how each of us was thinking of the other," Harriet said vaguely.

"Yes, it is," Matina replied, but the idea suddenly dawned on her that perhaps her mother wasn't suffering over her—perhaps she had some other bad news, some suffering over someone or something else. Maybe her brother, Eric. Or maybe that new man she'd met in the spring, the one with the two little kids. Maybe he moved back in with his wife. Or perhaps her mother's job was in jeopardy—state cutbacks, Republican belt-tightening. "So Mom, have you seen that guy—Rick—lately?" Matina asked, remembering again how her mother had hurt her. At moments she believed her mother had become attached to the unborn baby.

"Tell me about *you* first," Harriet said, glancing around the room, and Matina scrutinized her mother's face and believed she could read her thoughts: The apartment was chaos; Adam had been so orderly, had such a "humanizing" impact on her; why did she have to break up with him? At heart her mother had wanted her to marry Adam, have the baby, keep a neat apartment, and learn to cook. Matina knew she was exaggerating, but not a lot. Last winter her mother had given her a file box with a label on top: "Our Family's Best Recipes." She was ready for the immune system, ready to take a detailed health history on a real-live patient— and her mom gives her recipes for sweet-and-sour string beans and chicken with tarragon. Her silent rant made her smile, cracked her hard shell. "Oh Ma," she said, "I think you really liked Adam."

"How are *you*, darling?" Harriet asked again.

"Fine," Matina said patiently. She picked up the roller and started blotting over the orange streaks.

Harriet glanced at the open textbook. "You were studying?"

"Yeah, the complications of pregnancy. Toxemia, stuff like that.

Spontaneous abortion." She knew she was making her mother squirm, and she felt bad.

"I'd like to help you paint," Harriet offered, "so you can get back to your studies."

"I don't know if I have another roller."

"If you have a brush I can do the window frames."

She turned down the offer because her mother would make the job more complicated than it was. "Ma, something happen today?"

The cat was whimpering behind the closed bedroom door. Matina flicked the switch on the David Byrne tape. Her mother had asked for it off. Said she couldn't take the sound right now. The cat's meows escaped her notice.

"What's bugging you?" Matina asked.

"Trivial stuff. If I tell you, it really won't add up," Harriet said, her voice tired.

Matina felt a twinge of sympathy for her mother sitting opposite her with her silly pumpkin pin. But Harriet was reluctant to explain what had happened. It had to do with a plan for getting together with a woman she'd met last spring at a conference about changing careers. The woman, Paula Palladino, a photographer, had liked her and promised to get in touch so that they could talk at greater length. After months she finally called and invited her out to a Spanish restaurant, a place that served tapas, those wonderful little appetizers. "Tapas," Harriet said, then stopped abruptly.

"Ma, just go ahead."

Her mother explained how she and Paula Palladino had made plans to meet at Paula's apartment at 4:30, have drinks, then go to a terrific Spanish restaurant. "I was looking forward to the tapas." Her mother paused.

Well, what happened? Did the restaurant run out of tapas? Her mother reminded her that the story would sound nonsensical.

"Please go on," Matina urged, as she rolled out the creamy white paint, eclipsing the orange streaks. Meanwhile Carlos's whining grew louder.

Harriet sat bolt upright. "What's that sound?"

"I found a cat at the laundromat. Now about the . . ."

"You have a cat?" Harriet murmured, sighed, and continued. "The gist of the whole thing is that by the time I got to Paula Palladino's apartment, it was as if the woman had forgotten why she'd ever wanted to get together with me. Her phone was constantly ringing and she was answering it—talking to people with names like Natalya, Sheng, Roberto, Ivan. She was on a conference call with the world, while I waited and waited for her."

Matina had finished the white walls and stepped into the kitchen in order to wash out the roller. "Ma, go on, I can hear you from here." Harriet continued. "Finally Paula let the answering machine take the calls and went into her bedroom to change her clothes—while I *waited* some more. She came out ten minutes later dressed to the nines. And we went out, supposedly heading for the restaurant with the famous tapas. But you know where she took me?" Matina appeared in the doorway.

"To the Copper Kettle for hamburgers?"

"Close, Matina! To Peking Gardens."

"That old run-down place!"

"Yes, but I wouldn't go inside. I said, 'Paula, I thought we were going to a Spanish restaurant.' 'Oh I'm so pressed for time,' she said. 'I must have forgotten to mention the lecture at the museum at seven-thirty . . . and the service at Toledo's is so damned slow.' Matina, I could barely keep from crying. I was shrinking to the size of the Rolodex card she had probably made out for me. At the 'Changing Careers' conference I was important, big, a Renaissance woman; now I was expendable."

"It probably had nothing to do with you," Matina said.

"It hurt my feelings, honey. I do have feelings. Sometimes you sound so coldhearted."

Matina apologized and explained that she was just trying to figure out why her mother was so affected by this Paula character who sounded like a bimbo. Meanwhile Carlos, parked on the other side of the bedroom door, was whining. Her mother tried to hide a look of apprehension but couldn't.

Matina opened the bedroom door and Carlos sprang forward, heading straight toward Harriet, and circled around her, leaping onto her lap, settling down and closing his round yellow eyes.

"What did I do to deserve this?" Harriet asked, inspecting the cat but not touching him.

"Isn't he sweet?" Matina murmured. "But go on with your story. Did you dine on moo-goo gai pan?"

"No. I told her, 'I'm going to Toledo's; if you want to join me, fine,' and then I turned around and marched across the street and went to Columbus Avenue. Paula never came."

"Good riddance!" exclaimed Matina.

Harriet glanced down at the sleeping Carlos, finally touching him. "Matina, look at your pussycat. He likes me."

"Did you ever get your tapas?"

"I did, and they *were* delicious," and her mother described the spicy little tidbits—the tiny dishes of meat and sauces, and fish, and olives—in detail. "I even had two glasses of Spanish champagne."

"Is that the end of the story?" Harriet nodded. "Ma, you should be proud. You were decisive. You didn't let yourself be controlled by Paula Palladino." She always tried to praise her mother's assertiveness.

"It should be the end, but it wasn't. There's more . . ." she hesitated, but Matina urged her on. "The odds are so against this kind of thing happening in New York that I'm reluctant to tell you. You'll think I'm a nutcase."

"No I won't, I promise." She was now quite curious.

"I changed my mind. I don't want to talk about it. It's painful," Harriet acknowledged. "It shouldn't be but it is." Matina waited patiently, and finally her mother continued. "Your father and Marianne came into the restaurant, an amazing coincidence; but they didn't see me—also rather strange. I tried to ignore them but I couldn't. They were gazing at each other and whispering and touching each other. Marianne seemed downcast but your father was as tender as he could be. He took her hand and held it on top of the table for about ten minutes. He started kissing her fingertips."

Matina squinched her face in disgust. "They were probably on their way back from a fertility specialist."

"What makes you say that?"

Matina shrugged. "I'm sure that Marianne must be desperate to have a baby and, anyway, that neighborhood is a beehive of obstetric offices."

"Your father seemed so interested in her, so attentive."

"Yes, it *is* hard to watch," Matina said, glancing at her mother, then looking away.

"Your father was actually comforting Marianne. It made me sad," she said quietly. "I guess I always kept comfort at arm's length." And even more quietly: "I suppose I wanted to be understood, not comforted."

"What's wrong with comfort?"

"Nothing," Harriet replied, her gaze remaining on Matina. "But I think you're sort of uneasy with it, too."

Her mother's comment slowed her down. Perhaps they were similar in that way—drawn to the difficult path even when the obvious, easy one would do. No, she reconsidered—they were not alike. And if they were alike, she didn't want to think about it right now. "Ma, you've had a hard day. Don't make more out of it than it was. You were feeling left out, peripheral—that's all."

Harriet stared across the room into space, then her eyes scanned Matina's desk with its open textbook. "I wish I had one area of enormous competence, or a great talent that would be like a wave that would carry me forward. I don't. And now I think I'm fading."

Matina's mouth curled down as she glanced at her mother. For a fleeting second she was sure that her mother was talking about wanting a grandchild. That would be the gift. "Mother," she said strictly, "you're being silly."

At that moment Carlos shivered awake and stood up on all fours on Harriet's lap, then jumped to the floor and raced into the bedroom. Matina wanted to do the same. Her mother was rambling now, growing ever more self-doubting and uncertain, and Matina recoiled from the display, hoping she'd never succumb to those particular symptoms. Physicians were so different. Physicians knew what they knew; they were kind but they were authoritative. She marched into the kitchen and began to sauté chicken livers.

"Carlos has the longest cat whiskers I've ever seen," Harriet called in.

"I think he's adorable," Matina said loudly. "I rescued him. He was homeless and hungry."

"Can I help you get this apartment squared away, honey?"

"Not really, Mom. I'll have to retouch some spots in the morning."

For a few minutes each of them was quiet. Standing in front of the stove, pushing chicken livers around with a fork, Matina thought about her mother's words, *I'm fading. Fading* hardly described Harriet who always had, if anything, a certain radiance. She slid the pan off the heat and went back into the living room. Sitting down on the couch next to her mother, she said, "Ma, you're in a very strong position," and she advised her to concentrate on work, on its creative possibilities, on the specific—and she emphasized *specific*—contribution she could make. She touched her mom's arm, looked her in the eye. "You're an administrator. You're a V.I.P. You're going to get a big promotion. You're on the cutting edge of an important new field—recycling. You're making more and more public appearances. Be proud! You're a policymaker. Your program is setting the standard for communities across the country."

"Matina, sometimes I start thinking about all the things that threaten our environment, not just solid waste." Sighing, her mom launched into a minilecture about the enormous coal reserves in China and the fact that there were more fossil fuel reserves than ever imagined ten or fifteen years ago. "Do you understand what that means for the greenhouse effect?"

"Garbage, Mother! Garbage. Stick with New Jersey's eleven million tons of garbage per year."

"That's amazing, sweetheart. You remember the exact tonnage!"

Matina moved back to the tiny kitchen. "Are you hungry? Do want some chicken livers?" Harriet shook her head. She was still full from tapas. In fact, she claimed to have heartburn. Matina handed her some Maalox, then set the plate of mashed chicken livers on the living room floor. "Chow time, Carlos!"

"They look delicious," Harriet said. "You're becoming a good cook. Why don't *you* have them instead of giving them to Carlos?" Matina shook her head, and her mother smiled softly.

"Ma, I'm taking off in a while. I've got a date with a pediatric resident I met last week—at the hospital cafeteria." Her mother, disappointed, had hoped to lure her back to Weehawken to stay overnight, have brunch in the morning, take a few hours off from her books. "I wish I could go with you, but I can't," Matina said. "I have this date and an important exam on Monday. Actually I think you should sleep here tonight! I'll only be gone an hour or so." Matina called Carlos again, and headed to the bedroom to find him. "Chow time, Carlos!"

Her eyes inspected the small room. Flat on her stomach, Matina searched under the bed, under the dresser. Where was he? She pushed and hurled clothes and shoes and boxes around in her closet. "Mom," she wailed, "I can't find him."

"I'm sure he's here," her mother said, "Where could he go?" Harriet moved the couch and raised the sheet that Matina had used as a drop cloth. She looked under and behind the desk. Perhaps he was hiding on the top of the bookcase or in the cabinet under the kitchen sink. Matina checked. She inspected the bathroom, pulling the shower curtain back expectantly, but Carlos wasn't in the bathtub. "He's jumped out the bedroom window," she said, staring at the open window, then raising it as high as it would go and leaning out. Matina felt the life draining out of her own body. There was no meowing from the street, and she couldn't see a thing. The window was a black hole. Her life was vacant, dead, and powdery like a planetary landscape. Dry, dry . . . shelves of grim textbooks full of wretched disease. The body, a cathedral of death.

"Let *me* search your closet," her mom offered. "I'm sure . . . he couldn't have leapt out the window."

"I'm sure he did; and I'm going out to look for him," Matina announced. Her mother insisted on going with her.

Matina scoured the length of the block in front of her building. Nothing. Anxiety stung her. Her mother suggested they look in the alley and then walk up to the corner and around to the avenue and back on the other side of the street.

"Carlos, Carlos . . ." both of them took turns calling. Passersby were indifferent.

"He's gone," Matina moaned, and her mother thought they should give it one more shot and try heading in the opposite direction. She experienced a moment of hope: Carlos had headed back to the laundromat where she'd originally found him. "Maybe he has loved ones who still live at the Laundromat, Ma." Her mother nodded and put her arm around her. It was dark, starless, chilly. She didn't mind the weight of her mother's arm. Her mother—and even her father—loved her so much, too much; and realizing that made her feel like crying for them, poor losers, poor darlings.

The laundromat was bright and lively, with dryers turning, clothes tumbling and twisting, washing machines bubbling. Carlos wasn't there. "Did you happen to see a medium-sized solid-gray cat with a white bib and three white paws?" Harriet asked a young man folding clothes. "No," he replied, "but I saw an orange one."

On the way back to her apartment, Matina didn't feel like talking. Her mother said, "You won't like this idea—but you could get another cat, sweetheart." She didn't want another cat but she was too worn out to get angry. Only Carlos would do, no other cat. She was tired.

They passed a late-night deli-grocery store. Her mother offered to buy her a quart of ice cream. She declined. The brightness of the store frightened her. *Poor darling, poor darling,* she thought.

Outside the building she had trouble finding her keys. Her hands were shaking as she fished through her shoulder bag. She could tell that her mother's patience was wearing thin. All they needed now was to be locked out and have to track down the telephone number of the elusive superintendent. Finally she let her mother search her bag, and within seconds Harriet had located the key ring.

The apartment smelled of paint, was more chaotic and cluttered than Matina remembered, as if in their absence it had been robbed and ransacked.

"Look," Harriet said, "the chicken livers are gone! Carlos is here—I knew it!" Her mother's voice had a silvery ring.

A great weight lifted from Matina, as though a jaws of life had rescued her from inside a crushed vehicle and she could breathe again and move her limbs, and no vital part was missing. She went into her bedroom. She saw him on the middle of her bed, waiting. His eyes were open—round and buttery yellow. Shutting the door, she buried her face in his soft fur and breathed. She could feel the tiny thumping of his heart. Then she cried, making sure her mother couldn't hear. She cried and cried, all the while holding back any sound that might have betrayed her. She froze the sobs before they could escape, and her throat ached.

Finally calm, she opened the bedroom door to find her mother sitting stiffly on the couch, as though on a vigil. "Ma," she said, "sleep in my bed. I'll be fine on the couch." She scurried around the bedroom, tidying up, straightening the bed, putting a fresh pillowcase on the pillow. She found a large, clean white T-shirt that her mother could use as a nightgown.

"Who is this guy anyway, this pediatrician. Nice?" Harriet asked as she slipped off her suit jacket and began to undress.

"Sweet," Matina said; "and he'll be good with kids. He actually likes children."

"What's his name?"

"Derek." She paused a second or two. "Derek Dodge." She hugged her mother and kissed her and noted as she always did in the past year or two, how soft her mother's cheeks were. They seemed to be getting softer and softer, like fine old silk.

"Have fun," Harriet said lightly.

"Will you be okay here?" Matina asked, suddenly embarrassed by her disorder. "Do you want something to read? The TV is working."

"I'll be fine, really."

"There's beer in the fridge, also soda and some yogurt and orange juice," Matina said as she pinned her plastic ID card to the lapel of her white jacket and threw on a rain poncho and headed out the door for the hospital.

The streets were quiet, eerily empty; stores closed. She walked fast but without fear, as though her tiny ID were an enormous shield that would protect her from every possible danger. Inside the hospital, past the night guard, she inhaled the building's fabulous scent, a blend of vinyl floors and wax, disinfectant, formaldehyde, and mashed potatoes. She listened to the hum of the hospital, the almost-audible current of healing. She had no plans to meet a second-year pediatric resident, no date with anyone at all.

At her locker she picked up her stethoscope and draped it around her neck, put her reflex hammer into the pocket of her white jacket, and hurried to the staff cafeteria. She bought a plateful of food and a cup of coffee and carried her tray to a table half-filled with residents and interns. Because she was only a second-year medical student, they paid no attention to her, but she didn't care. She loved listening to them talk and laugh, and when they cracked jokes—terrible ones and good ones—about overwrought patients and bad surgeons, about unnecessary cesareans and botched abortions, unaccountable hemorrhages, about life and dying, she tried to laugh, too. And presently she felt the gaze of one resident, and could tell from his tired eyes that she'd gotten it just right: Her laughter carried the right mixture of respect for the body, for life itself—and knowledge of its less than perfect outcomes.

Discipline and Will

Two weeks after Eric got the lead in the ballet *The Prodigal Son,* he began to worry. His voice on the phone sounded tight and jittery. Everything was going wrong. He and the girl who was the lead ballerina were working at cross-purposes. A certain cold manipulativeness was required for her part, a headstrong abandon for his; neither one could quite bring it off. Moreover, he couldn't convey the *contrition* that was required for the powerful ending.

His voice grew loud and cruel as he imitated his teacher. "'*Contrition,* Eric! I want to see you crawling on your hands and knees! Crawl, Eric!'"

In a telephone call a couple of days later, he said, "Mom, what do I know? I've never had to crawl in my life."

I assured him that he wouldn't have gotten the part if his teacher had any doubts about his ability to do it: a mother's heartfelt sentiments.

"You're so sweetly naive," he said. "Politics enters into who gets the big parts. You wouldn't understand . . ."

"I understand 'politics,'" I countered. For almost five years I've worked for the New Jersey Department of Environmental Protection, in solid waste management; recycling garbage, to be exact. "Working for the state *is* politics."

"Okay, let's just drop it, shall we?" Eric mumbled.

At the point when Eric felt more confident, a few weeks later, he wanted all of us to attend the performance—his father and his father's young wife, Marianne; and his father's mother, Grandma Belle; and his sister, Matina, of course; and my boyfriend, Rick, and me. And we all wanted to go. We were captivated by Eric's ascent to excellence. He wasn't a Baryshnikov, and perhaps never would be, but he was getting better than anyone ever thought he would. His father loved his stamina, and his sister loved the muscles of his thighs and the power that was unleashed from them, and I loved his fine posture.

Discussing arrangements with Eric, I said, "You know that if your father and Marianne come, the baby comes, too."

"No *prob*," he said, a lilt in his voice. "I'll find a student who'll baby-sit."

I realized that he saw the baby as a bundle of entertainment, saw his father as a father again and not simply as Marianne's attentive husband. But the baby tipped the balance for me. I had become a far-off moon to new, more radiant planets.

Phillip, my ex, and I spoke several times and worked out the complicated plans, a process we were quite good at for a divorced couple. I'd drive my car to North Carolina with Rick, Matina, and Belle, who was afraid of flying, and Phillip and Marianne and the baby would fly. For the sake of convenience, we'd all stay at the same motel.

Then the night before leaving, late, Rick called. He couldn't go. His five-year-old daughter had come down with a hard-hitting virus and a fever of 103.6. "I can't go without you," I pleaded. "You'll be fine," he said, but I didn't feel fine. The journey to Eric would be all effort and arrangements, trying to keep everyone happy. Everyone needed to be handled with care.

For part of the trip Matina sat in the backseat of the Toyota with her grandmother discussing big-name designers—Isaac Mizrahi and Carolina Herrera and Franco Moschino. I always had trouble understanding Matina's love for Belle, who was prouder that her granddaughter occasionally did fashion modeling than she was that Matina was a medical student. For hours, it seemed, as we drove down the Atlantic seaboard, Matina and Belle talked about the right shape for fingernails, the comeback of loose face powder, and the scandals of the world of fashion. "I think my favorite designer is Giorgio Armani," I offered at one point, but my favorite designer—the fact that I even had one—didn't impress them. According to Matina I was too "spartan" to have a *feel* for fashion.

"In order to like fashion," Matina explained, "you have to be able to tolerate conspicuous waste and rapid obsolescence, and let's face it, Ma—you don't like waste. Your work has to do with eliminating it." "Transforming it," I corrected, and Matina laughed. "We'll have to find you a designer who recycles second-hand clothing," she said good-naturedly, and went back to talking with her grandmother. When she began enumerating brilliant designers who had died of AIDS, Belle grew quiet. AIDS was confusing and terrifying to her; it didn't happen to people she knew.

AIDS terrified me also. I had my concerns about Eric who'd told Matina he wasn't gay but that being a dancer, a lot of his teachers and friends were. His favorite male ballet teacher was dying in a hospice in Washington, D.C. His modern dance teacher from last year had recently tested HIV-positive. In due time Matina leaked bits of these conversations to me. If Eric wasn't gay, I still worried that perhaps he'd experiment once or twice, or give in to the overtures of one of his teachers, a person who might use flattery and promises to tempt him.

I could hear Belle snoring now and I pulled into a rest area so that Matina could get in the front with me. Washington was behind us and we were whizzing south through Virginia, and being in Virginia made me remember those years Phillip and I had lived in Richmond, years when the children were small and we weren't thinking about the environment or AIDS, when we took nighttime walks and tried to nose out whether the nearby spice factory was producing cinnamon or cloves that day. Having small children helps you see the world in a kinder way: You have to keep making sense out of it; it's your duty; and so in a way, you benefit from the sunshiny picture you've colored for them.

Try as I did not to have illusions about Eric's dancing, it was sunshine for me. I've watched Eric stretch and mold his body into a dancer's physique, with that miraculous dignity that dancers have. Their perfection seems to defy human frailty.

I was speeding along thinking that things had reversed themselves, that some of the light from Eric and Matina's lives was radiating through me, when Matina, who was doing a rotation on outpatient pediatrics, said, "Ma, did I tell you how I almost walked out of the clinic when Dr. Moss insulted the mother of a baby girl with an ear infection? I ask myself, *Will I be that way someday? Careless and insensitive?*"

I found myself wanting to defend Dr. Moss, wanting to protect myself from whatever disillusionment Matina was experiencing with medicine. "Try not to judge so harshly," I said.

"The bottom line is that you owe it to your patients to be compassionate and respectful."

How could I disagree? So I agreed and fell silent.

"I wonder how the baby did on the flight?" Belle said softly, sighing and yawning herself awake. Once over the North Carolina state line, even in the dark, I could feel Belle come alive and her energy pull up and out of the car and beam itself toward her son and Marianne and the baby.

At the motel, Belle immediately found out that her son and his new wife had already checked in, and she marched off to find them. Matina and I got settled in our room. Eric wouldn't join us till the next day because he had an evening rehearsal.

"I need to do some studying," Matina said after we had staked out our beds and made ourselves comfortable.

"I'd like to read for a while, too," I said. I was in the middle of a seventy-page pamphlet about new concepts in waste-to-energy incineration. However, Matina and I had no sooner started reading, when Phillip and Belle knocked at the door. Phillip was holding the baby over his shoulder and Belle grasped her son's free arm. The pajama-clad baby clung sweetly to my ex-husband's shoulder, an elaborate epaulet. They entered the room slowly, like royalty. Phillip, in a coral-colored cotton shirt and gray linen trousers, sat down in the armchair, the baby in front of him against his stomach. He made the obligatory thank you's for my driving

Belle. No, that's not fair. He was truly appreciative, truly happy we were all together. He kissed the baby's head, and ran his fingers along the baby's plump arm. I turned away but couldn't stop a solid wall of seawater from rolling toward me, turning me weak and breathless.

"So what do you think of this little guy, Harriet?" Phillip asked me at last.

Another wall of seawater crashed over me. I could see that Phillip was going to serve me up this baby. He rose out of the chair and lifted him onto one hand and carried him toward me as though he were a waiter breezing across a dining room with a tray full of dinner plates.

"He's adorable," Belle murmured, watching her baby grandson sail across the room.

Matina glanced up from her book. "Hi Dad, hi Greg," she said without fanfare, cheerful, I imagined, because Marianne had already gone to bed.

I had no choice but to take the baby from Phillip, or let him fall on the floor. For a moment I felt dizzy. My words were garbled. I tried cuddling the baby against my breasts and under my chin, but the baby's back stiffened and he arced away from me. I made jolly clicking and cooing sounds but they didn't come out sounding playful. They sounded like radio static.

Uncannily Matina stood up and took the baby out of my arms. Like Eric, she seemed to have recovered from her disapproval of her father's recent foray into parenthood, and actually got a kick out of Greg. Or perhaps the baby meant she could more easily ignore Marianne, who had in the past required too much attention. Marianne's efforts to be fair and reasonable with everyone in our family demanded more admiration than I wanted to expend.

Matina jiggled Greg in her arms and then stretched him out flat on the bed next to me and undiapered him. She lifted his thighs up and back so that he looked like a fat little frog. She checked the rotation of his hips.

"Is he all right?" Belle asked. There were times when Belle mistook Matina for a full-fledged doctor.

I admired Matina's competence and sweetness with Greg, aware that Phil was still waiting for me to say something about the baby. Even though I was the one who had officially left Phillip and was prepared for the fact that he would of course remarry, I was caught off guard by the baby, that he was such an incredible magnet for everyone. A strange light-headedness overcame me, a blurry unsteadiness, and, saying "he's lovely," I explained that I'd left something in my car.

The night was hot, the air smelled of fresh tobacco. I took the long way around the parking lot. My car sat alone, not far from the fenced-in pool area. I leaned against the hood and breathed the moist tobacco air and observed how the underwater lights illuminated the pool, changing the water into gold and turquoise swirls around the lone swimmer doing laps. I stared at the pool and saw plum, silver, sky blue. Color from where? I looked up to see if the water was reflecting lights from the sky, but the sky was uniformly dark and starless. I would never again have a baby.

The next day involved waiting; waiting for Eric to meet us at the motel after his last morning rehearsal, and waiting for the performance in the evening. The effort it took to be patient worked a spell on us all. We spread out on comfortable chaises around the pool. Belle parked herself under an umbrella midway between

Phillip and Marianne and me, a move of surprising diplomacy. Matina had offered to take care of the baby so that her father and Marianne could have breakfast alone—which they had done, and now Marianne was knitting a complicated cable-knit sweater for Eric. In my heart of hearts I wanted Marianne to stay away from Eric. I'd seen her ogle Eric's strong dancer's body; she was too young to be his stepmother. Besides, she had a child of her own to care for now. I prayed for a sense of humor, fair-mindedness, a sense of proportion.

I reminded myself of several things that sunny June morning: that it had been my decision to leave Phillip, that Rick was turning into my lover *and* my friend—exactly what I believed would never happen, and that Eric's dancing was his gift to himself, not to me or anyone else.

Matina was strolling around the pool area jostling the baby on her hip. I reached out my arms for him. Marianne glanced up from her knitting. Her hands rested on top of the bulky sweater and she was staring at me and beyond me, an expression I read as mistrust. I put the baby on my shoulder, against my bare skin, and he sucked my shoulder. I walked around with him, moving out of Marianne's watchful gaze, knowing that this would make her uneasy, but I wanted to make her *have to* trust me. I walked around with the baby for a long time.

We were relieved when our star arrived for a big midday meal. Eric *glissaded* toward us, his arms outstretched as though he were going to crush us together in one gigantic embrace. He kissed his grandmother and then hugged me. I could feel my throat tighten and my eyes sting with tears. I hadn't seen Eric since early January, and I didn't want to let go of him. He pulled away from me so that he could greet his father and sister and Marianne. I had trouble watching Eric and Marianne hug, both of them so young and slim, so exalted in their new careers: Eric's dancing; Marianne and her baby.

It was only later when I sat across from Eric in the restaurant that I realized how gaunt he'd become. His cheeks were slightly sunken and his nose had a razor-sharp reddish look, as though the cartilage was about to slice through the skin. He ordered a high carbohydrate dinner that would see him through the performance that evening, but when it came he ate slowly, without appetite. Very quickly the veneer of his warm greetings disappeared, and I felt his nervousness ticking away like a time bomb. He warned us that the ballet had never jelled, that it had been miscast and insufficiently rehearsed. Matina took issue with that. "Eric, that's all you've been doing for months." "Five and a half weeks to be exact," Eric stated. His complexion had a dark, purplish hue, the color that raw cut potatoes turn when they're exposed to the air for a long time.

Marianne made a reassuring comment about the evening's event and moved the conversation into Matina's court. Matina willingly launched into an amusing account of an eight-year-old boy at her clinic with a pain in his foot and how she finally diagnosed a fracture of his fifth metatarsal bone. Eric winced and told his sister not to mention foot injuries lest she jinx him. There was more small talk, but it was finally Belle who was the honest one. "Eric," she said, "you've lost a lot of weight. Too much. You're much too thin." Eric put down his fork. "That's how they like 'em here, Grandma," he said. "We're just *MEAT*." His bitterness startled Belle who didn't know how to respond. She didn't know what being *meat* meant.

"Let's let Eric eat his dinner in peace," Phillip said, but Matina persisted in reporting recent research about the downward trend of ballet dancers' weight. "We're seeing serious malnourishment," she lectured; "bone loss, other complications . . ." but Eric wasn't listening. He picked at his baked potato. I glanced at Phillip, whose good color and appetite were in cruel contrast to Eric's. His hand was resting on the back of Marianne's neck. I remembered when Phillip's hand had rested on the back of my neck, and how heavy it had felt, but Marianne looked happy. She had withdrawn into the private oblivion of nursing, and I envied the fact that she could nourish *her* child.

The food was lovely. Matina had veal with strips of red pepper and mushrooms. We ate quietly for a while and then I told a joke I had heard at work about garbage, and everyone laughed. We decided not to have dessert right then but to have it after the performance.

On the way out of the restaurant I overheard Belle say to Matina, "You know, Matina, they wouldn't even let Eric be a model: He's much, much too thin." "You're right, Grandma," Matina replied, "except that Eric doesn't need to be a model. He's a dancer." "He's becoming a superb dancer," Marianne added, and I could hear in her voice the same belief in Eric's extraordinariness that I was feeling. It was as though his talent would make us all soar. We'd become lighter, full of grace, restored.

Alone with Matina later in the afternoon, I said, "Something's going on with your brother. He looks emaciated. Is he on drugs? Cocaine?" Matina straightened and moved around in front of me, blocking my path. She didn't say anything; she rolled her eyes. "I don't care if you think I'm crazy," I insisted, "something is wrong." "I guess it's possible," Matina said, at which point I shivered.

•   •   •

In telephone calls from Eric during the preceding weeks, he'd mentioned certain demanding leaps that he had to perform in the first several minutes of the ballet, and the defiance and bravado those leaps had to convey. He'd referred many times to the terrible risk of falling flat on his ass. And so now, waiting for the curtain to go up, I could scarcely look at the stage. Nervously I rolled up my program, unrolled it, practically destroyed it. The family had filed into one row of seats, even Marianne who had cold feet about leaving the baby with an unknown sitter. The auditorium was packed: sparkling, attentive young people, parents on edge, faculty members trying to appear casual and confident.

The student orchestra began to play and the curtain went up. Within moments Eric bounded onstage. I forced myself to keep my eyes open. He jumped. He jumped high in the air. He landed solidly on his feet and smacked his fists against his thigh with all the cockiness of youth. Jumped again. No problem. Fine. I exhaled. I sighed. Then, whatever fear I had left disappeared as I was drawn into the duet of Eric and his partner, the seductive siren.

I could hear how splendidly the students played Prokofiev's music. I noticed the stage set, a luminous blue backdrop and a skyline of the biblical Near East, with its domes and minarets. And on my right, Matina was lovelier than I had ever seen her, in a summery floral-print dress her father had given her, her hair pulled back off her face the way I like it—in a single thick French braid. And sitting on Matina's other side was her father.

The duet continued and the prodigal son was encircled and overcome by the siren, who twined her long legs around him, a spider encircling her prey. A gnomelike troupe of revelers whirled around Eric in a frenzy of drinking and wild camaraderie, and then they left my poor son in a stupor; he was a rag doll, a sack of flour, a hopeless case. The revelers flipped him upside down and shook out his money, and the siren ripped the gold medallion from his chest. Out of the corner of my eye I saw Phillip reach for Matina's hand, and I was tempted to reach for her other hand but I imagined a powerful current looping its way through us and jolting poor Matina out of her seat.

The dance approached its finale. The prodigal son crawls back to his father's home—in shame; yes, in a state of excruciating contrition. The music is funeral-like in its dark, steady beat, and Eric's suffering, as he crawls and pulls himself across the stage, is convincing. I can barely stand it, his nose and belly to the floor, the intensity of shame, his pathetic thinness, his almost frightening concentration. His suffering is too real, his shame too real. Stand up, I want to shout. Eric, I beg you—stand up!

Lo and behold, the father comes forward to greet him. He raises him, and holds him cradled in his arms like a baby. The father cradles his almost-grown child in his arms and forgives him.

After the applause and the curtain calls, waiting for Eric, the five of us jammed the aisle, first swaying toward the stage, then toward the back doors, back and forth, searching for him all the while fielding compliments from Eric's friends. Phillip and I veered into a kind of self-congratulatoriness that as divorced parents we rarely allowed ourselves. Our son is talented and disciplined, our eyes signaled. Even Marianne and I hugged, and I realized that the one thing Marianne admired me for was for encouraging Eric's dancing. She was, I think, as mystified by his transformation as I was. None of us ever expected that not terribly graceful fourteen-year-old junk-food lover to become so good. And Belle asked each one of us: "How did Eric get to be that advanced?" and Phillip kept repeating, "Discipline and will, discipline and will!" I had never seen Phil so vibrant. He was bowled over by Eric's discipline and will. Belle nodded; she was as proud as the rest of us, but then she murmured, "Maybe it's too much of a strain on the boy." Matina was quick to say, "Grandma, of course work is a strain, but it gives you something to sharpen your eye teeth on . . . it gives you your place in society." Phil intervened gently. "Grandma hardly needs a lecture on the meaning of work right now." Belle disagreed. She always liked hearing whatever Matina had to say—she had such interesting ideas. Matina flashed her father a malicious little smile, but I could see in that exchange of looks that something between Matina and her father had changed. She had relented. She had finally forgiven him for Marianne and the baby.

We met up with Eric at the reception in the theater lobby, and he looked jubilant. Traces of makeup remained on his forehead and jaw, his eyes sparkled. His teachers and friends were congratulating and hugging him, shaking his hand, touching him. I could see that this was a school where there was a lot of touching. I scrutinized the males to see if one of them was Eric's lover. I observed a hug that went on too long. That was one of Eric's dance teachers, I assumed. A few moments later Eric introduced me. Lewis. Lewis hugged *me* too long also. Perhaps Lewis and Eric weren't lovers. Beautiful young girls with long swan necks glided by me, their bodies painfully thin and breastless.

"Mom, I did it!" Eric exclaimed, with his fine posture, his sweetness. I put my arms around him, kissed his cheek, which was clammy. We all took turns congratulating him while he whispered, "It's over."

Matina linked her arm with his, and the two of them moved into the crowd of young people. They stopped to talk to a young woman with a cello case. She was Asian—Korean perhaps, with waist-length shining black hair. She gazed at Eric with admiration. With more than admiration. Phillip escorted Belle and Marianne to the table where a couple of students were serving fruit punch. I stood alone. Rick wasn't there, but at this moment I believed that he cared about me. I pretended he was with me, his arm around my waist. I glimpsed Eric pointing me out to the tiny Asian girl with the cello case. I waved, and shyly she returned the wave. Eric and the Korean girl hugged, their bodies melding. My fears about Eric receded. This was a joyful occasion. I felt calm and at ease.

When the celebration at the school died down, the family headed back to the motel. Eric drove with me, the others in Phillip's rental car. Eric was no longer elated. I could feel his gathering gloom, and it frightened me all over again. "What's wrong, honey?" I asked. No response. We walked silently from the parking lot to the restaurant, past the fenced-in swimming pool. The night was humid and hot, and again the air reeked of fresh-cut tobacco. The parking lot was packed with cars that gave off a steamy heat, like a herd of jungle animals gathered to rest for the night. Eric sighed. "I can't wait to get to sleep," he mumbled. I tried to take his arm, but he pulled away from me. I was stung. Friendly physical contact was second nature to him.

It took a while for the family to gather. We waited for Marianne to return with the baby. Matina looked around the dining room impatiently. Colorful reproductions of famous paintings hung on the wall and tables were covered with crisp yellow tablecloths. Eric played with his spoon, silent, distracted, thin. The black shirt and pants he was wearing didn't help. He sipped water and glanced around the table like someone who was preparing to make a public address. Or an announcement.

Marianne finally returned with the baby wrapped tightly in a flannel blanket. No one was in the mood for announcements. Our appetites had returned and we wanted dessert.

When everyone had gathered, his voice barely audible, Eric said, "I have something I want to say." I pretended I hadn't heard him. No one wanted him to speak. We wanted to celebrate, we wanted to make toasts, we wanted to congratulate each other on various good performances. "Let me say this first, Eric," Phillip said, "we were absolutely impressed by your performance. You did an incredible job."

"Everyone did an incredible job," Eric said tonelessly.

"Yes, the orchestra, too," I said, thinking of the lovely cellist with the shining black hair. "I had no sense that the orchestra wasn't as good as any professional orchestra anywhere," I rambled, trying to take up time.

"No one wants to listen to *me*," Eric said, sipping more water, whiny. "Of course we want to," Marianne said. She shifted the baby to her shoulder and gave Eric her full attention, ready for his precious words as though he had good news to give us.

"Go ahead, Eric, shoot," Matina ordered. "What's the *prob*?" Eric was on the verge of speaking but the waitress appeared to take our orders. She enumerated what seemed to be an endless list of desserts—pecan pie and cheesecake and black forest chocolate cake and carrot cake—and finally jotted down our orders and left.

"So what's up?" Matina repeated, aware that Eric was into serious business now.

"Are you having trouble with one of your teachers?" I asked. I wanted to ask questions, even silly questions, in order to take up more time. I was dreading the worst.

Eric shot me a look of disgust. "It has nothing to do with how I'm getting along with anyone. I should've told you before you all came rushing down here; I'm sorry, my timing sucks. But here goes: First of all, I don't want to stay at this school. . . ."

"What?!" Phillip exclaimed loudly, then regained a measured calmness. "Are you kidding?! It's a great school."

"I haven't finished," Eric said angrily.

"There's more?" his father asked, with sarcasm.

"I don't want to stay at this school and I don't want to be a dancer."

"I don't believe it!" Phillip was shouting now.

"Isn't it obvious why!" Eric said, and I was sure I knew why. "Because of your health," I said knowingly, and Eric glared at me. Then he grew thoughtful. "I guess you could say that in a way. You see, dancing is great, that's true—but it has a sick side."

"So does everything," I said, and Phillip nodded heartily in agreement.

Eric ignored us. "I'm tired of hating my body for what it *won't* do. I'm sick to death of thinking about my body. The only relationship I'm allowed to have is with my own body." His voice grew angrier and stronger. "I want more for myself than being a trained seal. I want to eat normally and party and play soccer on a Saturday afternoon without worrying that I'm going to hurt myself. I want to love my life. I want to . . ."

I listened to him and sadly I didn't believe a word he was saying. My mind played tricks. I discounted what he said as though it were a preamble—and waited for the worst. I loved him so much and waited for the worst.

He went on repeating himself, a well-rehearsed litany. He was sick of being treated like a piece of meat. He was sick of being hungry. Sick of pain. Sick of orthopedists. He knew nothing about history or current events. He didn't know that much about the Vietnam War or how Germany got divided into East and West in the first place. He was sick of being a body that could only dance. "I want an ordinary kind of life. I don't want a career that ends when I'm thirty-two."

Belle turned to me and whispered in a voice loud enough for everybody to hear. "I never asked him to be a ballet dancer. In fact, I never loved the idea. Why is he so angry?" "I'm not sure I know," I answered, and noticed that Phillip was scowling. "You don't need to scream this to the whole restaurant," he told Eric, and a second later he said, "You were so incredibly good, you've had so much discipline. We've marveled at what you've accomplished in the last year or two. Let's not come to any conclusions now."

"Eric," I said, "why don't you tell us what's really wrong? Are you ill? Or is it something to do with your friend, the cellist?"

I detected a melting look in Eric's eyes, but then the melting look hardened to exasperation. "I don't have a health problem." He paused, glancing around the table at each one of us. "Dancing isn't everything," he said slowly.

Phil took the baby from Marianne and started patting him on the back, a trifle too hard. Marianne looked afraid. Belle leaned sideways staring at the floor, searching perhaps for a fallen napkin. No one could speak. Even Matina, who was never at a loss for words, was quiet. No one could say, *Sure that's perfectly okay, Eric. Stop dancing. Dancing isn't everything. You don't need to dance for us.* It might have been the right thing to say, but no one could say it. We were splintered again, separate, united only by the table, and the glasses and silverware and the half-eaten desserts. We loved

Eric's dancing, but the dance was over. And no one could say it was okay.

We were groping for some way to move beyond the moment. Matina was blank—no little lectures, no questions, no pertinent observations. Belle's features had gone slack. The baby now seemed to be staring at me expectantly with round, wide-awake blue eyes. Staring straight at me.

What did Eric want? His own life back, ordinary prerogatives? I took a deep breath and tried to signal my assent. Not easy. I had to tell myself that this dance hadn't begun and wouldn't end in the ways we'd been taught to believe. It had its own wild and frightening sort of beauty. I loved it and wanted more.

ACKNOWLEDGMENTS

My thanks to Mordicai Gerstein, Betsy Hartmann, Roger King, Marisa Labozzetta, Carol Edelstein, John Stifler, and the late Norman Kotker—current and former members of the Lyman Road writers' group, for listening and talking back. Thanks to Joe Olshan, my editor, for his guidance and amazing energy. I am blessed to have the encouragement of dear friends—you know who you are! And always, gratitude to Howard, my husband, and to Matt, Dan, and Rachel, my grown children, and Sue, honorary daughter, for their generosity and wit.

CREDITS

Selections from this work first appeared in the following publications. The author wishes to express her gratitude to the editors of these magazines and journals.

"Rain," "Charity Work," "What I Learned from Clara," "At the 'Changing Careers' Conference," in *New England Review*. "His Mother, His Daughter" in *American Fiction* (an Anthology published by Birch Lane Press). "Woman Made of Sand" in The *Boston Globe* Magazine. "The Madonna at Monterchi" in *Phoebe*, (under the title, "Her Honeydrop, Her Chickadee"). "Chicken Livers" in *Boston Review*. "Discipline and Will" in *The Virginia Quarterly Review*.

ABOUT THE AUTHOR

Joann Kobin's stories have appeared in *New England Review,*
Ploughshares, North American Review, The Virginia Quarterly
Review and The *Boston Globe* Magazine. Her work has been cited
in the Best American Short Stories and nominated for a Pushcart
Prize. She's been a MacDowell Fellow and has received a grant
from The St. Botolph Club Foundation in Boston and from the
Massachusetts Council of the Arts.